NIGHTMARE PASS

Marshal Galen Trimble is a hero: single-handedly he brought down the Crigger Gang, ending the so-called 'scarecrow murders'. But years later when he's targeted by an unknown killer, resurrecting the same *modus operandi*, people speculate that a lost Crigger brother is exacting his revenge. Now, as Trimble's old riding buddy Jim Hannigan and his lovely partner are brought into the investigation, their mission to find the killer will unlock a door to the past that alters their own future.

LANCE HOWARD

◆

NIGHTMARE PASS

Complete and Unabridged

LINFORD
Leicester

First published in Great Britain in 2006 by
Robert Hale Limited
London

First Linford Edition
published 2008
by arrangement with
Robert Hale Limited
London

British Library CIP Data

Howard, Lance
  Nightmare Pass.—Large print ed.—
Linford western library
  1. Western stories
  2. Large type books
  I. Title
  823.9'14 [F]

ISBN 978–1–84782–128–7

Published by
F. A. Thorpe (Publishing)
Anstey, Leicestershire

Set by Words & Graphics Ltd.
Anstey, Leicestershire
Printed and bound in Great Britain by
T. J. International Ltd., Padstow, Cornwall

This book is printed on acid-free paper

*For Tannenbaum.
And for Uncle Herb and Uncle Carle, both of whom passed away on consecutive days during the writing of this novel*

1

When Lessa Trimble glanced at the wall clock a shiver trickled down her spine. She'd stayed at the one-room school-house far too long, correcting papers she should have finished hours ago. But her mind kept drifting, focusing on the fate awaiting her when she stepped through the door to her home, where he'd be waiting on her, that look on his face she had come to loathe. The look that promised she would pay dearly for not having his dinner on the table on time, for not scrubbing the kitchen spotless, for not catering to his every need the way a good wife should. Unless she got lucky and it was one of the nights when he failed to come home at all.

It would be her own fault he took his fist to her again. She was asking for the mistreatment. She was begging for it.

That's what pounded into her head each time he doled out punishment for her transgressions. Lies she had come to accept as gospel.

At least until those moments when she lay safe in another's arms . . .

The redolent smell of ink and tang of fresh paper suddenly made her stomach turn, but she knew it was only the memory of the scent of her own blood filling her nostrils, the gunmetal taste of it on her tongue after he beat her, making her ill. Fear did things to a body: it rose sweat on her brow and made her pulse throb in her ears. It set her heart racing like horses stampeding and her hands trembling, as she lay a sheet of paper atop the stack of others on the huge pine desk.

Two weeks ago Lessa Trimble had celebrated her thirty-first birthday, but already her brown hair, pulled back into a tight bun, was frosting with gray at the temples. That too, along with the simmering fear in her soul, was *his* fault, though she supposed she should have simply accepted the blame for that as well.

She still kept her figure — Lord knew Galen Trimble would never let her go to tallow, as he so righteously put it. He wanted his woman — or should she say women? — to retain their youthful shape. How would it look for the town hero to keep a matronly wife? How would it look for him to exhibit anything other than a trophy worth his stature and standing? Horses or women, it made no difference. Both were owned in his view.

That was the reason they remained childless. Children made women fat, slovenly. He'd told her that as if he'd been reciting it straight from the Good Book itself. Decreed by God, women should stay sleek of figure, ready to serve. He ignored the edict 'be fruitful and multiply' because it wasn't to his advantage, didn't fit in with his lofty delusions. He brooked no argument on the point and denied her her earthly and heavenly right as a woman to bear a child. She rarely brought that up anymore, because he often enforced painful measures protecting against such possibilities. And to backtalk him meant harsher punishment, then usually a violent hour's worth of his using her in a 'husbandly' way.

'Bastard . . . ' she muttered, a spike of fury and terror plunging into her belly with the thought of his rough hands groping her, his sour breath from that rotgut whiskey he drank searing her nostrils. Every manly scent about him now repulsed her where once it had aroused like fine musk. Now he simply stank, but the odor came from his soul.

She stood suddenly, unable to control her shaking limbs. Moving around to the front of the desk and staring towards the door she wrapped her arms about herself, shivered. Her hands bleached as she tried to squeeze herself tighter, stop the shaking, the fabric of her blue gingham dress straining against her ripe bosom. The room was stuffy, too warm, yet still she felt incredibly frozen.

Her gaze drifted from the door to the rows of desks, the children long gone home, the gentle sounds of their laughter and sight of their bright faces one of the few joys in her life. She missed them, looked forward to the time she was here, teaching . . . away from him. This school was as close as she had ever come to having young'uns of her own.

At least until three weeks ago, when she discovered she'd gone far longer without her womanly than she should have.

Two days ago she'd begun to feel sick in the morning and found herself vomiting after Galen left for work. Other signs should have made it obvious, despite her fearful self-denial, but she knew with that sense only a mother feels what was growing inside of her.

He'd kill her if he knew. Another shiver. Her blue eyes shimmered with tears that went unspilled.

He didn't want children, that was certain, and it went beyond the fact she might lose her youthful shape. He carried a deeper motivation, and she knew it, though he would never admit as much to her. A child would mean the mighty Galen Trimble would have to come second in her life and second in the eyes of the town. The attention he craved would be siphoned from him with the arrival of a child. Folks would stop by to visit the infant, to see her, and offer their gifts and congratulations, while he looked on. They would offer him their well-wishes, too, but not because of something he did for them, something that made him all-powerful and virtuous in their eyes. It would be second-hand adulation, intolerable to a man such as he.

No, Marshal Galen Trimble, savior of Hollow Pass and lone vanquisher of the Crigger Gang would never stand for that.

Pitiful. If only he realized he'd been

living off the currency of his reputation for longer than its value. Folks simply feared him now, though that distinction escaped him. They didn't respect him, but he was too bound to an image of what he once was to figure it out. An image that may well have never existed anywhere but in Galen Trimble's mind.

A sob escaped her lips, shook her body. A tear slipped from her eye, but she quickly brushed it away with a sleeve. No, Galen Trimble would never tolerate her telling him she was with child. If he didn't kill her for the news, he would the moment he figured out the child could not possibly be his. With the means he took to avoid such possibilities that would not take more than a few moments.

She'd been seeing someone. Secretly. The affair started out of spite, she supposed, something to pay him back for those saloon women he lay with — everybody in the entire town knew of it, for God's sake, and how she detested their looks of pity when they knew he wasn't watching. But something had changed soon after she met a man at the general store; he'd helped her load supplies for the school onto her buckboard, then offered to follow her and help unload. A kind man, he owned the livery stable. What had begun innocently enough with Clavin Pendelton had quickly taken a turn to the more tawdry the day after Galen beat her for ruining a shirt with a hot iron. She'd run to Clave for comfort and ended up in his bed.

It was wrong. She knew it. All her moral upbringing raged against such sin, but she couldn't stop herself. Was it so bad to have all her emotions returned, all her passion reciprocated? Was it wrong when the man she wed didn't love her and mistreated her so, slept with other women? Made her believe she was to blame for every goddamned thing that didn't go his way?

Yes, and no. It wasn't as black and white as her Bible schooling made it all seem.

Clavin was such a gentle man, his touch caring, his concern genuine. He made her see life had more to offer than going home to an ogre day after day. Made her feel she was worth more than being one man's porcelain whore.

Clavin had begged her to leave Galen, go with him somewhere, anywhere that wasn't Hollow Pass. But how could she? He would kill them both. So she had told Clavin no, she was chained to her fate and that was that. It was better this way, because at least then the man she truly loved would be safe from Galen's wrath.

And life would go on, each glance stolen, each wish stillborn.

But now she had little choice. She'd begin showing soon. Her breasts were already aching, straining against the fabric of her dress. Any other man not so wrapped up in himself would have noticed by now her frequent trips to the watercloset.

Your decision's made, she assured herself. And maybe that was the double blessing of this child growing in her belly. It gave her strength to do what she dreamt every night of doing. She and Clavin had discussed it. They'd made plans, picked new names. In two days time it would all be over, if she could only keep her nervousness from showing so much she gave herself away to Galen.

Clavin had purchased tickets on a train bound for the east. Once they left Galen would never find them. He would look, certainly, pry under every rock and scour every corner searching for his wife, his possession. But after a time he would give up, go back to his whores. Then maybe after a few months or a year she could stop living in fear and bring her baby into a family that was safe and filled with joy and love and caring.

But she had to stop making stupid mistakes like staying too late at school, if she were going to pull it off. She was placing not only herself but her unborn child in danger, if he beat her again.

Another shiver. She had better get home and face him. She didn't want to. God in Heaven, she didn't want to.

Two days. The waiting was the hardest part. It gave her too much chance to fret and fear.

'Soon,' she whispered, rubbing her belly. 'It'll be over soon. It's the only way. It's the *best* way.'

She went to a hook on the wall, grabbed her shawl, then wrapped it about her shoulders. She could put it off no longer. The preternatural dusk would soon be upon the small Colorado town as the sun slipped behind the distant mountains. The walk to their home was not long, but it led down a wooded trail shadowed by forest and if he wasn't already on his way to come looking for her he soon would be. Her only chance at avoiding his wrath was in reaching home before he did and pretending she had been there for the entire time.

She went to the door, opening it, then stepping out into the late-summer day. The air carried a sultry quality, moist and uncomfortable, or perhaps it was simply the sweat dampening her skin making it feel that way.

She locked the door and turned, freezing instantly, a gasp escaping her full lips. A figure sat atop a black horse, staring down, silent. At first glance she saw Galen's face on the figure, then quickly realized that was only her over-wrought imagination.

For the figure on horseback had no real face to speak of. His features were covered by a black sacklike mask, holes cut into it to reveal small brown eyes that glittered at her with the strangest of looks, one that seemed to pry into her very soul. A mouth stitched in thick yellowish thread gave the mask a scarecrowlike appearance. A black duster covered most of the man's average-sized frame and ebony silk shirt, flowed over the top of his black trousers. Black scuffed boots jammed into stirrups completed the figure's peculiar ensemble.

The figure said nothing, merely kept

looking down at her, as if struggling with inner thoughts. She trembled, afraid to move, worried she might lose her senses and collapse into a dead faint if she did.

At first unable to make her voice work, she finally managed to get words out. 'W-Who are you? What do you want?'

The figure didn't respond immediately. His cold gaze continued to hold her in its spell. Deciding, that's what he was doing, she concluded. The figure was weighing a decision, if she read those eyes right, one that would seal her fate.

'I'm . . . sorry . . . ' he said a moment later, voice a grating whisper.

'What? Why? Who are you?' Her voice jittered, riding a scale of crescendoing terror.

'It'll be easier if you don't resist,' the figure said. 'I promise to make it quick.'

'What do you want? Did my husband send you to frighten me?' Her words came in a frantic stream and her gaze jerked to the trail that led towards town. It lay many yards across a browning lawn that surrounded the schoolhouse, but reaching it was her only chance. Yet even then she knew she'd never be able to outrun a man on horseback.

The figure uttered a low laugh, its tone holding not a hint of humor, only mockery. 'Your husband ... ' He leaned forward slightly. 'You might say he sent me, but not in any way you or he'd rightly expect ... '

She had no idea what he meant by that, and didn't care. Fear got the better of her and she forced herself to move. With a sharp sound of terror, she burst towards the trail, highlaced shoes kicking up dust as she ran along the walkway, then across the grassy yard.

Behind her she heard a 'Yah!' as the figure kicked his horse into motion.

Reaching the hardpacked trail, she ran, not looking back, forcing her legs to pump as hard as she could. Whatever her husband was, whatever cruelty flourished within him, this figure was something worse, something terrible. Death rode that horse. Death that had come for her for some reason she couldn't begin to fathom. It had something to do with Galen, something that had finally caught up with him, but that was all she could guess.

She stumbled, her toe hooking an upraised root. The ground rushed to meet her and she thrust out her hands, flesh scraping from her palms as they skidded against the solid earth and small pebbles embedded into the dirt.

Tears flooded her eyes as she suddenly thought of the child growing in her belly. Her life meant little, but that baby . . . that baby deserved the chance to live, grow, become all she never had.

The thing on horseback skidded past her, unable to stop the animal's forward momentum. She looked up to see the figure jerking to a halt, reining around. The horse neighed, a great black beast as frightful as the figure riding it.

'No,' she murmured, pushing herself up to her feet, spitting dust, trembling. She bolted into the woods that lined the trail, diving into the lush clumps of brush and stands of cottonwood and maple, pine and spruce. Branches clutched at her dress, tearing a swatch from her sleeve and drawing a streak of blood on her flesh. She stumbled along, leg muscles burning, threatening to give out. A great crashing came from somewhere behind her and she let out a startled bleat. He was following, on foot.

Barely able to catch her breath, she pushed herself harder, but her progress seemed only to slow as exhaustion turned her limbs to lead and brought nausea to her belly.

She wouldn't make it much farther. The sounds of the thing behind her grew louder. He was gaining.

'Please help me, Lord in Heaven, please . . . ' she mumbled, heart pounding so hard she thought she would vomit it at any moment. A branch whipped her face as she chanced glancing backward. She glimpsed the figure, about twenty feet back, coming on like the Spectre of Death. Coming for her.

For an instant, the thought the Devil had sent his minion after her for her transgressions with another man stabbed through her mind. But, no, this was no demon, no creature of the supernatural. It was merely a man, dressed like he was for some reason she would never know.

The woods seemed to grow darker, branches interlacing overhead, choking off the waning sunlight. All other sounds seemed to stop, the chatter of birds and forest creatures, the shushing of the wind — all sounds except the pounding of her heart and throbbing of her pulse.

Closer.

The clamor of his thrashing through brush loudened and she uttered a soft scream.

It can't end this way, she told herself. It can't. She couldn't let him take her child.

Something grabbed at the back of her shoulder. She jerked away, part of her dress tearing, tried to make herself run faster.

Her legs were gone. Sheer momentum propelled her now. She dared not look back, because if she did she would see him there and freeze in terror and he would have her.

'Noooo!' she screamed, panic flooding her veins. 'No, please, don't!'

Then he had her. Gloved hands grabbed her shoulders and upset her forward thrust. She went down, hitting the ground hard, branches slicing at her face and clothing.

Gasping, she tried to struggle up, but the thing in the mask was on her, wrenching her shoulders around and slamming her flat against the ground.

'Don't resist, Lessa . . . ' the figure said, cold eyes boring into her fear-stricken own.

'Whatever he did, it wasn't my fault . . . ' she said, voice barely audible.

The figure paused, as if struggling

with something in his own mind. 'I know . . . '

He reached for a knife in a sheath at his waist, drawing it slowly.

She screamed, knowing there was no hope, no chance at redemption for her miserable life and no chance of a future with a man she truly loved. The blade glinted as the figure jerked it above his head, then brought it down in a powerful thrust. A prayer died on her lips as searing pain pierced her throat.

★　★　★

Clavin Pendelton finished up the paperwork he'd been meaning to get to for the past week. It wouldn't look good leaving things in poor order when he left in two days, would it? No, it wouldn't look good at all. And he did so like to have all his chickens in a pen.

Sitting behind the desk in the small office at the back of the livery, he ran a hand over his angular chin and leaned back in his seat, finding it difficult to concentrate on his work. Her face kept drifting into his mind, her lovely face. His thoughts meandered to the future he had planned for them in Atlanta. She was having his child and he couldn't be more proud, more hopeful.

And more scared.

If that sonofabitch husband of hers found out before they left . . .

Jesus, the man was the town marshal, for godsakes. A local hero, least in his own eyes. Maybe he had been at one time but now he was nothing more than a power-hungry bastard, and, in Clavin's estimation, a dangerous one.

Two days. That's all. Just two short days. They could keep things hidden that long certainly, though he harbored suspicions they might have been seen together by a couple of the townsfolk. They had been careful, but total secrecy was impossible in a town as small as Hollow Pass. The marshal had spies everywhere, those who hoped to curry favor, despite their dislike of his heavy-handed authority.

But they'd be gone by the time word got around. He hoped.

Clavin was not a large man, in fact, he was what most folks just called wiry. A hair past five-seven, he had ropy muscles and a ruddy freckle-peppered complexion. Blue eyes reflected worry under reddish eyebrows and a thatch of carrot-colored hair. Most women wouldn't have given him a second look, but Lessa was different. She saw past the outer trappings of a man, looked into his soul and formed her judgment based on what he was made of. In him, she had seen all he felt for her, that his very being lived for her alone.

Under any other circumstance he would have chastised himself to hell and back for getting involved with a married woman. It was plain wrong, Bible said so.

After a spell he had come to justify his — *their* — behavior by the fact the man she lived with was a monster. Galen Trimble treated the loveliest woman on God's Green in a way no human being should ever be treated. And while that didn't relieve the guilt, it made it bearable.

Anger worked itself into his veins and his face reddened. If only he had the guts to confront Trimble, tell him he was riding away with his wife and that was that. If only he had the guts to put a bullet into that lowly sonofabitch.

But he couldn't do either. He was no coward, but the marshal wasn't a forgiving man and had a temper few in town wanted to cross. Least those he hadn't run out. And Clavin Pendelton couldn't hit a barn door with a gun to save his life. He'd practiced some, the notion of ending Trimble's life playing in his mind more than once when Lessa told him what that man had done to her. But killing a man was nothing to be taken lightly, and Trimble would likely out-draw him in a heartbeat.

So secretly leaving was the best way.

A noise from the livery beyond the office pulled him from his thoughts. He looked out through the large window into the stable proper, but saw nothing. He wondered whether one of the horses might have made the sound, but he had long ago relegated their nickering and shufflings to background noise and that wouldn't have alerted him. This stood out from that, like a footfall, deliberately set down extra hard.

He stood, a bolt of apprehension traveling along his nerves. What if Trimble had found out, what if he had come here to —

You're being ridiculous! he told himself. Making a mountain out of a gopher hill.

Still, he couldn't shake the feeling someone was out there, waiting for him.

He went to a gunbelt hanging on a hook embedded into the wall behind his desk. Easing a Smith & Wesson out of the holster as if it were some coiled snake, he clutched the weapon in his grip, its cold steel comforting, yet repugnant. He'd never really gotten used to the way everyone carried guns out here. It wasn't like that in more genteel Atlanta.

He edged towards the door, heart stepping up a beat. Opening the door, he drew it inward and peered out at the row of stalls. He heard the normal sounds of the horses, as well as voices and the rattle of buckboards filtering in from the street. The familiar musk of dung, old leather and hay filled his nostrils.

'Anyone out there?' he called out, trying to keep his voice steady.

Silence answered.

His nerves were getting to him. That's all it was. They'd been sneaking around, worried about exposure for so long, a trigger reflex had embedded itself into his system. Trimble didn't know about them and that was that.

He let out the breath he'd been holding and forced himself to relax. The gun lowered.

'Pendelton!'

The voice came from nowhere, yet everywhere, cracking like a blacksnake whip, and Clavin swore he came nearly a foot off the floor at the sound of it.

'Who's there?' he shouted back, gripping his nerves, sticking his chin out.

No answer. He shuddered, despite himself.

Stepping out into the aisle of stalls, he peered about, seeing no one and wondering where the voice had come from. From the front, through the wide opened double doors, he saw an occasional passerby on the street. Through the double doors at the back he saw only the dusty back street lined with crates.

He started down the aisle, his hand gripping the Smith & Wesson tighter, sweat dampening his palms. A thin bead of it trickled from his forehead down his cheek with an annoying itch.

'Come on out, whoever you are. I'll call the marshal if you don't.' It suddenly struck him as a foolish thing to say. Last goddamn person on earth he wanted anywhere near this livery was Marshal Trimble.

Something slammed him in the back.

25

He bounded forward, unsure just what had struck him and sent him flying. The gun tumbled from his grip, landing on the haystrewn floorboards. He hit the floor an instant behind the gun, barely getting his arm before his face to prevent a broken nose.

Drawing a breath, he began to push himself back up. Someone grabbed him from the back, getting two handfuls of his shirt and hoisting him to his feet, then just as quickly hurtling him towards a stall door. He crashed into it, unable to get his feet on solid ground, or stop himself.

The blow stunned him, sent a cavalcade of stars sparkling across his vision. The livery spun before his eyes. He hit the floor again, this time flat on his back, and lay staring upward.

'You didn't really think you'd get away with it, did you?'

Oh, Christ, his mind thundered, recognizing the voice. He forced himself up to his elbows, shaking his head to clear the cobwebs. A moment later, the place stopped whirling and he saw the man standing there beside an open stall, where he'd likely been hiding, waiting until Clavin passed to fling open the door to slam into his back.

He knew, goddammit, he knew. That was the only thought Clavin was capable of forming for the next minute as Galen Trimble stared down at him, his dark eyes accusing, damning. Trimble was a large man, a bushy mustache hanging over his lips, dipping an inch to either side. The elements had etched his face with premature lines and too much rotgut had reddened his nose. His dark suit and tin star made him look like some sort of demon come calling. His beefy hand drifted over the grip of his holstered Colt, the way a mother would caress a child.

'Answer me, boy.' Trimble stepped forward, bootfalls like thunder on the prairie.

'I — I . . . ' he struggled to form words, his heart slamming at his ribcage. 'I don't know . . . '

27

Trimble's eyes narrowed. 'You don't know what? You don't know you been dipping your wick in my wife? That what you're sayin'?'

The revelation, though he knew it was coming, seared him like a scalding hot iron, branding him as an adulterer. Someone had seen them. Someone had told.

'I . . . don't know what you're talking about.' It must have been the wrong thing to say but he got no time to think on it. Trimble lunged, reaching down, grabbing handfuls of Clavin's shirt and hoisting him up. He slammed him against a support beam, pressing his face close.

'Goddammit, don't you insult me by denying it. I know you've been with my wife. The shopkeep saw you together, saw you touch her. He's too scared of me to lie.'

'Please, I didn't — '

'You best not have, or I'll come back and kill you.' Trimble jerked Clavin forward then slammed him back into the beam. It struck the back of his head and he felt liquid flow down his neck. His vision blurred, spun, and throbbing thunder boomed in his skull. Trimble hurled him again.

Clavin went head over heels, rolling like a ragdoll along the livery floor until he crashed into a stall door and lay gasping in a tortured heap. He groaned, trying to summon his strength to fight back, but his body wouldn't heed his will.

Trimble was on him in an instant, hauling him to his feet and jamming him against another beam.

'Admit it, that's all you gotta do. I can keep this up all goddamn night if you don't, but I reckon you got maybe one or two more blows left before the funeral man's taking you out of here in a box.'

Clavin stared blearily at his accuser, wanting desperately to deny it to the death. But terror and self-preservation got the better of him and words spilled out in mumbled lies. 'Yes, yes, but I swear I didn't touch her in a manly way. I swear, please . . . '

He prayed Trimble didn't hear the lie in his voice. The marshal's breath beat against Clavin's face, sour with whiskey, and likely that was the only thing preventing the lawdog from hearing the truth behind the words.

'That so hard, Pendelton?' The marshal's face got redder and Clavin was suddenly in motion again. He sailed through the air as if his bones were made of rubber. Had he resisted, tensed, the landing might have killed him, but he tumbled again like a circus clown doing a prat fall and came to a stop just inside the back doors.

Trimble laughed, stamped towards him like a Reaper wearing a tin star. 'I'm giving you one warning, Pendelton. I catch you anywhere near Lessa again, I'll come back and if I don't kill you you'll wish to goddamn hell I had.'

Clavin looked up, blood dripping from his mouth, eyes unable to focus entirely. He nodded a weak yes, knowing to do anything else was certain suicide. But in his mind he prayed he'd be able to ride in two days time and take Lessa away from the sonofabitch.

Trimble seemed to accept the answer, grinning, a vile expression like a leather-covered skull. The lawman tugged the ends of his vest down and pulled a watch from his pocket, checking the time. 'Well, well, reckon it's time I go let Lessa know you won't be seeing her no more, don't you think?'

A bolt of terror went through him but he saw nothing he could do. In that moment he reckoned he was a coward after all. He couldn't even ask the man not to hurt her. He merely stared, pain careening through every inch of his body, tears filling his eyes.

Trimble stuffed the watch back into his pocket and with a parting chuckle walked from the livery. Clavin struggled to get to his feet but could only fall back, panting, groaning, terror over what would happen to Lessa boiling in his mind but too impotent to do anything about it.

*　*　*

Goddamn woman. He couldn't believe she'd dare mess around on him. The gall of her, trying to soil his good name in Hollow Pass.

Galen Trimble rode along the trail leading towards the schoolhouse. Day was bleeding to dusk, the sun a memory now behind the distant Rockies. He'd stopped at home first, only to find that no-good Jezebel of a wife not there with his supper on the table. Again. By damn he wouldn't tolerate such insubordinance from anyone. He had never done so in his life, even from Clara long ago, the one woman he reckoned he'd ever truly had emotions for, and he wasn't about to start now.

She would pay dearly for it, and for stepping out on him.

He didn't really give a damn that her feelings might have gone to another fella. No, that wasn't it. He cared because he had married her for her looks and body, because a man of his stature deserved a possession such as her, to display for all to see. If she had disgraced him to anyone other than the shopkeep, who wouldn't dare say anything to anyone if he intended to stay in Hollow Pass, he would do more than simply give her a beating this time.

The more he thought it over the more anger flooded his veins. He should have told that idiot liveryman to get the hell out of Hollow Pass. Maybe he still would, unsatisfied now that he'd only given him a beating. What the hell did Lessa want with a skinny little red turd like that, anyhow? The woman was plumb foolish. She risked everything she had for a Nancy boy.

Galen Trimble was a hero in town, and in the West. Hell, pulp novels had been written about his triumph over the Crigger Gang. That made him a hell of a lot better than a liveryman.

He grinned, the thought tickling him.

Triumph, indeed. Old Trip would have rightly disagreed with that, but then again old Trip wasn't around any longer to tell the tale.

Those days were gone, and somewhere beneath the layers of whiskey rot maybe he entertained the notion he had run out of past glories. But the notion was fleeting, judged insubstantial and intolerable by the man he was. Just another will o' the wisp.

The schoolhouse was only a short distance farther. His hands tightened on the reins, anticipation of the confrontation with that cheating whore simmering in his belly. 'You best learn your place, woman,' he mumbled. 'You're mine and that's all there is to it. Ain't no other man ever gonna have you. I won't be disgraced in my own town.'

He grew aware he was talking to himself, something that happened when he indulged in too much redeye early in the day. But the day had been slow until the shopkeep came to him, so he had figured a few tilts wouldn't hurt. Half a bottle later it had taken him two hours to sober up enough to go after that liveryman.

Something ahead caught his eye, tore him from his thoughts. At first he couldn't believe what he was seeing and blinked, thinking maybe the whiskey was doing things to his vision.

He guided the horse closer, eyes narrowing, disbelief chasing away some of the alcohol haze.

'Jesus Christ Almighty . . . ' he mumbled.

He drew up, staring at the sight at the edge of the trail where it widened into the schoolhouse yard.

A woman's body hung on a crude crosspost, the kind used for scarecrows in cornfields. She'd been tied there, arms outstretched, clothing nearly torn completely off. Blood bathed her chest and belly, flowing down from where she had been cut. Her head slumped, hair pulled free of its bun and straggled across the features, but he didn't need to see her face to know it was Lessa.

He sat there for what seemed like an eternity but was only moments. No sympathy or grief for his murdered wife rose in his being. None at all. That she'd come to be in this position was likely her own fault, God's vengeance on her for even thinking of betraying her husband.

No, what went through him was a nascent fear that something from his past had come back to haunt him. This murder reminded him of a time long past, told him what had happened here had happened for a reason and was a message directly meant for him.

'Scarecrow . . . ' The word trickled into nothingness as he remained frozen in the saddle for another moment. With a sharp breath, he climbed from his horse and began screaming, fists clenched, against the outrage someone would perpetrate on him. How dare anyone come to his town and challenge him in this way. How dare the past ride in like Death's bastard horseman to spite the hero of Hollow Pass.

The rage soon passed. A grim smile appeared on his face. For with the notion someone had meant this for him he also saw how he could turn the sympathy of a hero losing his beloved wife to his advantage. The town would mourn, offer their condolences. The smile only got wider when he thought about the look on that idiot liveryman's face the moment he found out Lessa had been killed in this manner.

Galen Trimble laughed and returned to his horse, mounting and reining back towards town, leaving the body of his wife to the crows.

2

'You're gettin' mighty secretive with our cases lately. You still haven't told me where we're going or why. We're supposed to be partners.' The complaint came from a young woman atop a palomino. Dressed in a riding skirt, buckshot sewn into the hem to keep it covering her shapely legs, and a frilled blouse, her complexion hinted at her mixed Mexican heritage. Straight black hair glistened with a blue sheen under the brassy sun. Her full lips drew into an annoyed frown aimed at the man riding beside her.

Jim Hannigan sighed, wishing they didn't have to rehash the same arguments all the time, but knew the blame lay mostly with him, so he took it like a child forced to drink paregoric for the grippe.

Jim Hannigan's hazel eyes focused on

the trail ahead, his lined but handsome face showing no emotion, but his rangy frame stiffening ever so slightly. He would have preferred to send her back to his office, but after the events in Miller's Pass even that wasn't safe. When they'd returned to Denver after spending two weeks scouring the countryside for the trail of a brutal knife killer, they discovered his secretary had been murdered by a man Hannigan had once put away, a man now dead. He reckoned in their line of work, it wasn't safe for her anywhere, but at least if she were with him he had a chance to protect her.

Not that she wanted or needed his protection nor saw it as anything less than a slight on her abilities. She could take care of herself better than most men but that didn't stop him from worrying about her. He'd nearly lost her too many times lately.

'Don't s'pose I could convince you to stay some place safe while I take this one on myself?' A wry grin became barely perceptible on his lips.

She cocked an eyebrow. 'Don't suppose you'd like to spend the rest of the day revealing your reasons for wanting to keep me away from any action on these cases?'

She had him and she knew it. Tootie del Pelado was a quick study when it came to reading — and frustrating — Jim Hannigan.

Fact was, he'd reached an impasse. After what occurred in Miller's Pass he couldn't put off the decision much longer. He had either to let her in or push her from his life forever. Neither option brought a measure of comfort at the moment.

The day was warm, bleeding summer. That scent of approaching autumn haunted the air, a few leaves hinting at color, patches of grass browning. Nights were still pleasant but it wouldn't be long before a chill set in. For now, the fragrance of late summer flowers perfumed the breeze and birds twittered away in the trees lining either side of the trail. Small animals scurried through the brush, unseen, disturbed by the clopping of their horses' shoes on the hardpack. Somewhere nearby he could hear the trickle of a brook. Everything seemed so serene, belying the grisly event that had summoned him here.

Fifty yards further on, the trail opened into a grassy lane and he saw a small red building off to the right, a trampled dirt path leading to its door.

'Schoolhouse . . . ' Tootie gazed at the building. 'Looks deserted. Shouldn't kids be there this time of day?' She looked at him and he nodded.

'Reckon that's part of the reason we're here.'

''Bout time you told me, isn't it?' Her voice carried a harder edge. She wasn't going to tolerate his lack of sharing information much longer and he didn't blame her. He'd gotten away with it too often the past few months.

'If I had told you beforehand you might have put up a fuss.'

She glared. 'If I look insulted about

you drawing that conclusion consider yourself a master of the obvious.'

'Tootie . . . ' He drew out her name just because he knew it irritated her.

'Don't Tootie me. You know damn well I'll still object if I have a mind to, then do what I please anyway. Why put yourself through the wringer every time?'

She had a point. He pursed his lips, unable to dig up a decent comeback. He leaned forward, flipping open a saddle-bag and pulling a newspaper from within. He passed it to her without a word.

She eyed the newspaper, one hand on the reins, one flipping the paper open. 'Hollow Pass *Tribune*? Where'd you get it?'

'Someone sent it to me.'

'Who?'

'Don't have any notion. It came without a return address. No note either. But whoever sent it knew I would see the lead article and be likely to come.'

'For what reason?'

'Look at the headline.'

She gazed at the words, which read: MARSHAL'S WIFE MURDERED. Below, in smaller type: CRIME RECOLLECTS SCARECROW MURDERS.

'I don't understand.' She shook her head, then scanned the piece.

'The Scarecrow murders. Old news, except maybe in Hollow Pass.'

'Says Marshal Galen Trimble's wife was found hanging on a crosspost naked, her throat cut.'

He nodded. 'That's the way they operated.'

'They?'

'The Crigger Gang.'

'We're here after them? Did you know this woman who was killed?'

'I knew her in passing. Fact, I went to her wedding. The Crigger Gang, no, we're not after them, not unless we've become ghost hunters.'

'You aren't making a whole lot of sense. Maybe you'd best fill in the holes before I get more prickled at you than I am already.' She cast him a serious look that said he'd best stop dancing around things.

He might have laughed if she wouldn't have tacked his hide to a wall for it. 'I knew her husband, Galen Trimble. We rode together on some jobs for the Cattleman's Association in Texas. There were three of us, me, Galen and another fella named Trip Matterly.'

'This Galen's now a marshal according to this article.'

'Yep, he got himself quite a reputation after we went our separate ways. He always liked being the focus of attention, sometimes even got a little hotheaded and reckless about it. Fact is, I half-expected I'd be reading 'bout his death some day, not his wife's.'

'What about the scarecrow thing?'

'The Crigger Gang. They robbed more stages and banks in these parts than any four outlaw gangs put together. They wore masks, with stitched mouths and hollowed eyes, black dusters, so they looked like the Devil's scarecrows. They had a hankering for women, and a peculiar way of leaving 'em hanging in cornfields naked after they were done with them. They cut their throats, let the crows — '

'I get the picture,' Tootie put in before he could describe the scene any further.

'They were mean sonsofbitches. Galen, he got a notion to go after them and he let everyone know it through the papers. Stupid thing to do. Would have told him so myself, if we wouldn't have parted ways. Brought on some events that might have played different otherwise.'

'You part as friends?'

He shrugged. 'More or less. It was a little strained between us, 'cause I turned him and Trip down about going into our own agency together. I was mostly a loner, only took those jobs early on when I needed the money. But I told him he ever got himself into something too deep to let me know and I'd come help. He probably saw that more as an insult, now that I think back on it.'

'You do have a way with words.' She grinned, but her face turned serious a beat later. 'What happened with the gang?'

'They struck at him. He made himself a target, but what was worse was he made someone else a target as well, someone innocent.'

'This Trip fella?'

'I s'pose him. But mostly Trip's sister, Clara. Galen was engaged to her. The gang got her alone one night, did things to her no animal deserved. Galen found her hanging on a crosspost.'

Tootie's hand tightened on the reins, draining white. She looked closely at Hannigan, making him want to squirm in the saddle. He knew what she was thinking. She wanted to ask him if that was part of the reason he wanted to protect her from things on their cases, that he was afraid she'd end up like Trimble's fiancée.

He reckoned he owed her an honest

answer. 'Yes,' he said, almost a whisper, and she nodded, looking straight ahead again, a satisfied look touching her features because he had somehow read her thoughts and provided her with what she wanted to hear this time.

'Trimble went kinda wild, I hear tell. He and Trip. Trip was furious and grief-stricken. Trimble was just plain enraged. He tracked them down, killed all except one of them single-handedly.'

'And this Trip fella, what happened to him during this?'

'He was killed by the gang. Galen saw it happen, testified to it before a judge.'

'What about the one who escaped?'

'Joe Crigger. Last I heard rumor had him in Old Mex. Galen tracked him for weeks but never caught him.'

'You think maybe this Crigger brother's come back for revenge?'

'I don't know. It all happened a long time ago. Seems like Crigger would stick to hiding out and not risk getting a marshal like Trimble on his tail again.'

'Yet someone killed his wife in a manner like those old murders.'

Hannigan nodded. 'Someone . . . ' His brow cinched. 'Seems the obvious answer, don't it? Lone outlaw returns practically from the dead to get even. Crigger could have been in a jail somewhere all this time and just got out. So maybe . . . '

'That why we're headin' towards Hollow Pass — that *is* where we're headin', isn't it?'

'Yeah, that's where. Isn't much farther.'

'He asked for your help?'

'No, he doesn't know I'm comin'. But, like I said, I met his wife, Lessa. She was a decent woman who didn't deserve Galen's past comin' back on her.'

'He's this big hero marshal; don't you think he can handle it himself? He might not want our help.'

'He might not, but I don't aim to give him a choice.'

A puzzled expression played on her

face. 'Why are you doing this, Jim? You got another reason behind it. I know you.'

'Figured maybe I'd renew old ties, relive the old days.'

'Oh, please, like I've said a hundred times, you're a poor liar.'

He frowned. He hadn't quite expected her to pinpoint any ulterior motive he might have had. He wasn't sure he had one himself until she mentioned it, but maybe she was right. He had known Galen and Trip nearly ten years ago and there was always something about them that made him edgy, despite their friendship. He wasn't kidding when he'd told Tootie he'd half-expected to read about Galen getting himself killed. A man with a rep like that attracted hotheads trying to make a name for themselves. Hannigan had encountered that problem more than a few times himself. It came with the job. But Galen and Hannigan were opposite in one major respect: Galen courted notoriety, went out of his way to seek the spotlight.

Hannigan did his best to avoid it. He considered Galen's position a flaw, maybe a fatal one.

Why do you really want to go back? he asked himself. noticing Tootie still peering at him.

He searched his thoughts, finding a notion he didn't really like growing stronger the more he dwelled on it. He didn't want to tell Tootie the conclusions he suspected because they were groundless, mere supposition. He'd forgotten about them over the years, at least until that newspaper arrived. Now they were surfacing again.

'Jim, tell me. I deserve answers now.' Her voice held steady but gently demanding.

He nodded. 'Reckon I wasn't quite sure till you asked, but, yeah, there's something else. When the three of us worked for the Association things would happen, little things I never connected at the time. Some were just things that got under my skin, others . . . '

'What kind of things are we talking about?'

'Galen, he was always a ladies man, even while he was dating Trip's sister, I expect, but this was before they became betrothed. We'd be at the saloon sometimes after work. He and Trip dragged me along when I wanted to go off on my own. Galen would talk up our cases for the Association like they were some great pulp adventure to any bar-gal who would listen, which was all of 'em pretty much, because he was loose with his pay. 'Cept the stories always came out wrong, most putting him in the position of hero.'

She laughed. 'Sounds like regular menfolk braggin' to me.'

He nodded. 'Yah, mostly, but it went beyond that. Hard to explain. Trip and I didn't want the credit and Galen gladly took up the slack, made himself into a mythical figure by all accounts. You'd have thunk he was Wild Bill himself by the time he got done.'

'That can't be all that's draggin' you out here.'

'No, it's not. Money would disappear

sometimes from some of the ranches, sometimes even heads of cattle. I'd wake up and find Galen out of his bunk more often than not at night. I never thought much of it at the time, but Trip, you always got the notion he was thinking something he wasn't saying when he looked at Galen. They were an unlikely pair to hook up, but I guess Trip let go of whatever suspicions he had, because they rode together till Trip died.'

'No proof?'

'No, not even suspicions really back then. Maybe I just looked the other way because I didn't want to believe anything bad of him.'

'Still doesn't seem like enough for you to force our way into this case.' She passed the newspaper back to him and he returned it to his saddle-bags.

'No, it don't. But maybe it's just things that have brewed in my mind for too long have finally got to boiling over. I can't say why something strikes me as plain wrong about this, but it does.'

'And you got an idea it's tied in with Trimble, and goes beyond some simple revenge plot against him by a lost outlaw brother?'

He shook his head. 'Wish I could say yes definitely, but I can't. Maybe it's just an old debt I want to repay. I always got the notion Trimble was mighty irked because I didn't go in on that business proposition with him and Trip.'

'What did Trip think of you turning them down?'

'Trip, he was always a bit of a schemer. Saw him pull some underhanded things himself playing poker. Nothing that would get a fella shot, but he rode the edge. I got the feeling he was just as happy I'd turned them down. Think he saw me as a guilty conscience.'

He went silent, gaze locking on a crude crosspost jammed into the ground a short distance from the schoolhouse where the trail met the grass.

'Surprised Galen didn't remove it,' he muttered. Tootie looked at the structure, a frown creasing her lips.

'That where it happened?'

'According to the article.'

'What about the schoolhouse, what does that have to do with anything?'

He smiled, but quickly hid the expression before she noticed. 'Galen's wife was the local school teacher. Guess what part you're playin'?'

She cast him an annoyed grimace. 'You do that just to keep me from showin' my wares as a saloon gal?'

He didn't answer, but chafed at her figuring it out so easily. He really had thought he might get away with that one.

'You're jealous, aren't you?' she said.

Did his face color and give him away? Sure as hell felt like it did. And he damn well didn't care for that smug little twist to her lips.

When the hell are you going to learn, Hannigan? She's a woman; that gives her special powers to prevent a fella from getting away with anything.

He did the only thing he could think of doing: he ignored the question. 'You're to see a Mrs Apperby at the general store. She knows you're comin'.'

'She does, does she?' Tootie raised an eyebrow.

'You're registered at the hotel under the name Pauline Twily. You come from Texas and have taught children for one year.'

Her mahogany eyes narrowed. 'Pauline Twily? What the hell kinda silly name is that?'

'Sounded good at the time.'

'S'pose I'm stuck with it.'

'You s'pose right.'

'You had my bag sent to the hotel, I take it?'

'Arrived on the noon stage if all went according to plan. You'll ride in first. Galen doesn't know you, so I'd like to keep it that way. Don't rightly know how thrilled he'll be to have me there, so we best not be seen together.'

She nodded, her face showing she

plainly didn't care for it but at least it meant her involvement, so she would tolerate it for the time being. He got the feeling the bill would come due later.

They rode in silence until the town came into view beyond the trail. He nodded to her and she acknowledged the signal, gripping her reins tighter.

'Tootie . . . ' Words struggled to find their way out of his mouth.

Her mahogany eyes softened. 'Yeah?'

'Be careful.' His gaze focused on the still-healing scar on her jaw from their last case's close call.

'Ain't I always?' But she nodded, face somber. He knew she was thinking of the ripper case they'd been involved in a few weeks back, too, the murdered women, and her complexion lightened a shade.

He watched her gig her horse into a ground-eating gait towards the town. He drew up, giving her a few minutes to ride in.

This is getting harder, Hannigan. You'll have to decide this time. You've put it off long enough.

The notion weighed on his mind, worse since the events at Miller's Pass. Neither had mentioned the loss he suffered there, or the unfinished business between them. While he'd hidden his grief over Catherine from her, he knew she saw it anyway, in weak moments when sorrow filled his eyes. She respected him enough to give him the time he needed for that, the privacy, but she deserved her answer now. Things were coming to a head and if he chose her he would have to deal with a ghost from his own past.

Or he would have to leave for good.

'The lady or the tiger, Hannigan?' he muttered. In this case the tiger meant a return to his empty life until the day a bullet found his heart.

He sighed, kicking his roan into an easy gait. His mind turned towards the newspaper in his saddle-bags. Who had sent it? And why? Surely Galen hadn't. Hannigan didn't know how his old friend would receive him but inviting him onto a case surely wasn't it.

No, someone else wanted him looking into this, but who? Someone who knew of a connection between Trimble and himself? He would have suspected Trimble's wife, had her murder not been the catalyst for coming here.

The why of it had to be connected to the who. Once he found the answer to one, he had the answer to the other.

The trail opening before him, trees fell away into occasional stands of cottonwood, lone pines or spruce. In the distance he saw the slate-blue ghosts of mountains, capped with white, their peaks stabbing the clouds.

Hollow Pass was a small affair, Y-shaped with a few alleys and side streets. He noted a lone saloon, general store, bank and gunshop to the left, a mercantile and dress shop, marshal's office to the right. The livery stable was near the junction of the Y and he headed towards it, planning to make arrangements for his horse before checking into the hotel.

Passers-by scuttled along the streets, a few giving him a curious glance, then quickly turning away. They appeared oddly stoic, focused on whatever business they had in mind. But there was something else, a depressive quality to their stride and demeanor that puzzled him. The town seemed idyllic in many respects, nestled in the woodland, an abundance of cattle-raising land to the east, plentiful water and numerous mining opportunities. Denver was only a two-day ride. He saw none of the usual carefree prattle among the folks he might have expected in such surroundings. A handful of children scurried about, likely glad to be out of school, but even their faces seemed somehow . . . forlorn. Maybe that was the word.

'What kind of town you run here, Galen?' he asked himself under his breath.

The sudden levering of a shell into a chamber jerked him from his thoughts and he drew up, raising his hands. He'd been caught completely unawares and it sent a wave of chills rolling down his spine. Sloppy, Hannigan, he scolded himself.

He didn't budge, waiting for whoever held a rifle behind him to make the next move. If whoever it was wanted him dead he would have been right there and then. He practically felt the rifle boring into his back.

And this time Tootie wasn't around to pull his fat out of the fire.

3

'You best keep your hands where I came see 'em and climb down from that nag real slowlike.'

The voice came from behind Hannigan and he relaxed. Today wasn't his day to die.

'I reckon I might decide to try runnin' for it.' A trace of a smile creased his lips. 'Reckon you're too slow to catch the horse or see well enough to aim beyond twenty feet at your advanced age.'

A hardy laugh sounded behind him and he turned. It had been years since he last saw Galen Trimble, the day of the man's wedding, in fact. The lawdog had put on twenty pounds, though most of it looked to be gristle. The marshal had a rifle aimed at the ground.

Trimble uttered a sarcastic laugh.

'Keep up that kinda talk, you sidewinder, and we'll see who can outrun who!'

'Fifty says I can still beat you in the dash.' Hannigan dismounted, taking the reins and guiding the horse around.

Trimble scoffed. 'And another fifty says your horse can walk there faster than you can run.'

'Been a long time, Galen.' Hannigan, leading the roan, came up to the man, hand extended.

The marshal took it, his grip still powerful enough to bend a horseshoe. Hannigan matched it, recollecting Trimble respected no one who didn't exhibit a strong handshake. A memory came back to him. One of the ranchhands during their stint for the Cattleman's Association had gotten on Trimble's bad side for just that small thing. Trimble ridiculed the fellow, calling him a Nancy boy. He'd been careful not to do it around witnesses, though Hannigan had overheard him on more than one occasion. The 'hand finally got tired enough of it to simply ride off one night and seek work elsewhere, instead of letting Trimble bully him into a fight, which was just what Galen wanted — an opportunity to pummel the man.

'That it has, old dog. Last time I saw you, well, hell's bells, I think it was on my wedding day.' A strange look drifted across the marshal's eyes, unreadable, but it had something to do with his wife, Hannigan felt certain.

'Sorry for your loss, Galen.' It was all he could think of saying and it seemed sorely inadequate. Truth was, loss was something Hannigan had damn well seen enough of lately but he wasn't a man who put his feelings into words especially well.

The marshal nodded, mustache bobbing. Looking at the ground, he kicked at a pebble embedded into the hardpack, then looked back up. 'Yeah, well, that's the way life goes out here sometimes. We all seen our share of tragedy. You go on . . . '

Hannigan nodded. 'I was just about to board my horse at the livery, then get settled in. We'll talk a spell after.'

Another look came into the marshal's eyes and again Hannigan couldn't read it. The lawman seemed on the verge of saying something, hesitated, then came out with it. 'You stayin' long?'

'Not sure.'

The marshal nodded, face tightening a hint. 'I'll walk to the livery with you. After we'll head on over to my office, get ourselves caught up.'

Hannigan smiled and guided his horse towards the stable. They covered the distance in silence, the manhunter already feeling tension building between them. Same old Trimble, he reckoned. Although they shared a friendship of sorts, some unspoken competitiveness on Trimble's part always erected a wall between them, preventing them from forming the bond men naturally did out here in the West.

He led his mount into the stable, the musky aroma of hay and dung and leather drifting into his nostrils.

A man came from an office in the

64

back, stopping suddenly as he spied Marshal Trimble. A peculiar look washed over his face. Fear, Hannigan would have bet, but the man quickly hid it. A trail map of bruises and scrapes marred the liveryman's face, too many to have been accidental.

The manhunter eyed him as he came up to them. 'You been in a fight?' Hannigan asked, not one to mince words. He heard a small intake of air come from Trimble and the liveryman hesitated, eyes darting, as if he were trying to think of some excuse for the marks.

The man's fingers, trembling slightly, went to his cheek. 'Why, no, no, I just got too close to . . . ' His gaze avoided Hannigan's as he faltered. 'A mad horse. Horse like that, should have put him down ages ago. My own fault.'

No horse did that, and Hannigan caught a double-meaning behind the words. He glanced at Trimble's face, which held no emotion, though his gaze was locked on the liveryman. Whatever the case, Hannigan reckoned it was none of his business. It had nothing to do with the death of Trimble's wife and that was his mission here.

'Need two weeks board at least, I figure.' Hannigan pulled a roll of greenbacks from his pocket and peeled off a number of bills. 'You'll see to it he's got your best?'

The liveryman nodded as Hannigan passed him the big roan's reins.

After grabbing his saddle-bags and slinging them over a shoulder, the manhunter left the livery, Trimble following, still silent. They walked for a moment, Hannigan wondering just how to approach asking Trimble about his wife's death.

'How you been keepin' yourself, Jim?' The lawman broke the silence as they stepped onto the boardwalk and headed towards the marshal's office.

'Reckon I can't complain.'

Trimble cocked an eyebrow. 'Really? I heard things, you know. Your reputation's getting damn near big as mine.'

'It ain't somethin' I encourage.'

Trimble let out a scoffing laugh. 'Everybody wants their day in the sun, Hannigan.'

Hannigan shrugged. 'Someone tries to kill me every few weeks based on it. Reckon I could do without that.'

'Just don't let yourself get too famous. Or then I'd have to kill ya.' Trimble said it as a joke but something about his tone made it decidedly unfunny. Hannigan let it pass, but it pricked his nerves.

They reached the marshal's office, the big lawman entering first, Hannigan shutting the door behind himself.

After propping his rifle against a wall, Trimble went to his desk, lowered himself into the plush leather chair behind it, then tossed his hat onto the blotter. Hannigan selected a hard-backed chair and dragged it over to the desk. The office was large, with three cells lining the back, a rack of rifles on the west wall and a couple of expensive tables with ball and claw feet. A number of drawings of Trimble from newspapers had been framed and hung, as was a portrait he'd obviously commissioned. Even the coffee pot was a silver piece with fancy inlay and set on a silver tray. Trimble obviously didn't play the role of an austere lawdog.

Trimble eyed Hannigan, one brow slightly raised. 'Let's cut through the bullflop. Why are you here, Hannigan?' With an index finger, Trimble brushed his mustache away from his lips. 'I reckon you didn't suddenly decide you wanted to chew over old times after all these years.'

'Can't an old friend ride in and say howdy?' Hannigan tried a grin that didn't work.

'You never could joke, Hannigan. That's why I always got the ladies.' He paused. 'Anyhow, I ain't seen hide nor hair of you since my wedding day, now you show up out of nowhere. Surely it ain't coincidence.'

Hannigan gave a slight nod, figuring

Trimble had given him the perfect opening to bring up the murder. He dropped his saddle-bags on the desk top. Flipping the flap over, he pulled out the newspaper, then passed it to Trimble, who took it. 'That all true?'

Trimble's brow furrowed. 'Where'd you get this?'

'Someone sent it to me.'

'Who?'

'Wish I knew. It came without an address. At first I thought it might be you, but you were never the type to ask for help.'

Trimble grunted. 'You got that right. I didn't send it. You figure this paper was a call for help?'

'Someone wanted me to see what happened here, someone who either knew I had a connection to you or knows my reputation, and wanted me to look into it.'

'Wouldn't it have been a mite easier if whoever it was had just sent a telegram?'

Hannigan shrugged. 'Got a notion

there's a reason this someone didn't want it known he was involved unless worse came to worst and I didn't come. Then he'd likely have to reveal his identity to get me here.'

'He? Sounds like you got suspicions.'

Hannigan shook his head. 'Or she. Like I said, I got no idea.'

'I don't need help, Jim. I'll find who did this and bring him down. My poor Lessa deserves that much.'

Hannigan heard a curious lack of conviction in the statement, but folks handled their grief in different ways. He had lost track of Trimble for enough years to be unable to predict how the man might react to the loss of his wife.

'I'm here for a couple weeks, Galen. I aim to poke around.'

A glimmer of hostility sparked in the marshal's eyes, and his cheeks reddened a notch. 'Like I said, I don't need help. I'll find the bastard responsible.'

Hannigan ignored him, shifting in his seat. 'This smacks of the Crigger Gang's way of doing business.'

Trimble uttered a condescending laugh. ''Cept the Crigger Gang's dead. Brought 'em down myself after they killed Clara and Trip.'

'Except for Joe Crigger.'

A distant look came into the marshal's eyes, annoyed yet far off. 'My biggest failure as a lawman. I chased him halfway to Hell, I figure, but never got close enough to put a goddamned noose around his neck. Lost track of him near the Mex border.'

'You figure he might have come back, done this?'

'No . . . no, can't see that . . . ' Something in the man's voice said he was lying.

Hannigan decided to call him on it. 'Don't reckon I believe you.'

Trimble blew out a heavy sigh. 'Suit yourself. Hell, maybe he did decide to come back, who knows?'

'Mighty peculiar coincidence someone using their method against you, don't you think?'

'Like you said, men with reputations

like ours, we get folks trying to kill us every so often, trying to make names for themselves. Anyone could have read about my taking down that gang and how they used to operate. Whole pulp tales written about it.'

Hannigan nodded. 'Though whoever it was didn't kill you, he killed Lessa. Why?'

'Hannigan, you ask some damn strange questions. What's it matter? They killed her. Maybe they were lookin' for me and I wasn't available right then. Maybe they wanted to strike at me that way. Who knows? And it makes no nevermind to me. I'll find whoever did it and they'll hang just as high.'

Hannigan tried to read the man but couldn't get an accurate assessment. Trimble's voice still held a curious dispassion, except for maybe annoyance at the manhunter for forcing his way onto the case. 'I can wire a friend of mine from Pinkerton. See if anything new's turned up on Joe Crigger.'

'Can't stop you but think you're wastin' your time. If it is him he'll come sniffin' round again, likely to try for me next. I'll get him, then.'

'Damn shame . . . ' Hannigan's gaze locked with the marshal's.

'What is?'

'First Clara, now Lessa. A man don't deserve two such tragedies in one lifetime.'

'No shortage of misfortune in a lawman's life. Comes with the territory.' Again Hannigan heard no emotion over the deaths in the man's voice, saw no grief in his eyes.

'You had the service?'

Trimble nodded. 'She's buried at the cemetery, edge of town, few feet away from Trip, in fact. Why you ask?'

'Thought I might stop by and pay my respects. Least I can do.'

'Ain't necessary, Hannigan. Thought that counts. Fact, you really should consider turning around and headin' back where you came from. Really no need for you to stay around.'

Hannigan stood, closing the flap on his saddle-bags and slinging them over a shoulder. He left the newspaper on the desk. Studying Trimble for a moment, he didn't care for the feeling weedling into his mind. 'Why, Galen, I get the notion you really don't want me here. That any way to treat a friend who rode all this way?'

Trimble offered a forced smile. 'Hell, just don't want you wastin' your time. You got a notion, stay, try some of our local gals at the saloon, but don't bother lookin' for killers . . . '

The last part came with an edge. Had it been anyone else Hannigan would have immediately suspected it was a threat.

He moved to the door, gripped the handle, looking back at Trimble. 'I really am sorry for your loss, Galen. I've had some of that myself lately. It's . . . well, maybe it's changed something inside me. I'm starting to see things different, figure out what's really important.'

Trimble bellowed a laugh that immediately irritated Hannigan no end. 'Hell, you going soft as a gal on me, Hannigan? The mighty Jim Hannigan, a Nancy boy? Soon you'll be tendin' gardens and preachin' the gospel to the sinners.'

He fought the urge to take Trimble down a few pegs. The man had just lost his wife. 'Reckon there's no shortage of sinners at any rate.' He stepped outside, taking a breath to calm himself. Maybe he had made a mistake coming here. Trimble was the same arrogant s-o-b he'd always been, maybe even more so. Why bother giving him help he didn't want?

Because you're doing it for Lessa, and for whoever thought it important enough to send you that paper, he reminded himself. Because something's stuck in your craw from all those years ago and you always knew someday it would need finishing. And because maybe you see too many coincidences with the deaths of Clara, Lessa and Trip and the lack of emotion in Trimble's manner?

Maybe. Jim Hannigan had survived years because of his manhunter's intuition and right now it told him something was dead wrong here.

To that end, he'd left the paper on the marshal's desk on purpose. He scooted along the boardwalk, then crossed the street and stepped into an alley running beside the general store. From that position he could watch the marshal's office for a short time. If Trimble had any idea who sent that paper he wouldn't waste much time confronting the person.

Hannigan loitered fifteen minutes, starting to wonder whether he'd mis-judged Trimble or if the marshal had figured out he was being baited.

The question was settled a moment later. The marshal's door opened and something dropped in his belly. He had hoped he was wrong, that Trimble was just a cold man with nothing to hide. But the lawdog stepped from the office without even bothering to look about. He had the newspaper half-crumpled in his hand and a determined, angry look on his face. Hannigan eased back, watching the man stride along the boardwalk. He wondered where Trimble was headed, betting it wouldn't take long to find out.

*   *   *

Clavin Pendelton experienced only the slightest measure of relief now that Jim Hannigan had come to Hollow Pass. He'd heard of the man's reputation and knew from all he'd read of Trimble the two had associated at some point in the past. He had counted on that fact to lure Hannigan here when he sent that newspaper. It had been a long shot, but it was the only thing he could think of doing. Risking a telegram would have been foolhardy in this town, would have brought Trimble down on him, gotten him either beaten to a pulp or run out of Hollow Pass. Damn key-tapper wouldn't have kept his mouth shut; he was too scared of Trimble. The whole town was. He would only have chanced such a direct method had the manhunter not pieced together the summons.

Lessa deserved better than that sonofabitch had given her. Trimble hadn't bothered lifting a finger to look for her killer, and he never would. He'd spent the past nights in the saloon with that whore he favored. Nights that Clavin snuck off to the cemetery to kneel at her grave and weep like no man should ever have to.

But now that Hannigan was here, would it matter? Was Jim Hannigan the man those novels said he was? The man who delivered vengeance? And how could Clavin get close enough to the manhunter to talk to him without someone seeing it, without Trimble finding out?

Something else gave him doubt also. While Hannigan had been the only one of his kind Clavin could think of trying to hire, a chance existed Hannigan was no better than the lawdog and would side with Trimble, tell him that someone had approached him. What if their past association was a stronger bond than justice for Lessa Trimble? What if those reports of Hannigan were wrong and he was just as big a crook and heartless a bastard as Trimble?

It didn't matter. Clavin saw no going back nor did he want to. The other day Trimble had beaten the hell out of him, and like a lowly coward he'd whimpered away. Trimble could run him out of town or pound him into the hardpack but he wouldn't back down to him again. And he wouldn't let Lessa's death go unavenged.

Clavin finished forking straw into a stall and closed the door, setting the pitchfork against a post, then started back to his office. He felt better and worse at the same time. He'd pushed his luck with Trimble earlier when Hannigan was here. He'd figured Trimble wouldn't say anything at that point, and wouldn't be annoyed enough to bother coming back after him while the manhunter was in town. He could get away with things with the townsfolk under his thumb, but not with a newcomer, least not immediately.

In that estimation Clavin discovered he was painfully wrong because the moment he opened the door to his office his heart damn near stopped beating.

'What the hell are you doing here?' he blurted before he could stop himself.

Trimble swung his feet off the desk and stood, face ruddy with anger. 'Came in the back way while you were tending to Hannigan's horse. Figured you and me needed to have ourselves another talk. Apparently the last one didn't sink in the way it should have.'

'W-What do you mean?' Clavin felt scared enough to soil his britches, but stood his ground, didn't back from the office or try to run.

Trimble snatched a newspaper from the desk. The paper hadn't been there when Clavin left the office, so the lawdog must have brought it with him.

'You sent this paper to Hannigan, didn't you?' Trimble's eyes were practically a slit and Clavin saw fury within them.

Clavin's belly plunged and he felt frozen where he stood. 'I-I sent no paper.' His voice jittered; he started to tremble.

A cruel smile filtered onto Trimble's lips. 'Ain't no use denying, it, Pendelton. You're the only one stupid enough in this town who could have. Don't know how you figured out he'd come running to help an old friend, but now I gotta deal with the mess you made. I ain't particularly happy with you, you know that, Pendelton, don't you?'

'I didn't send it.' The lie in his voice was obvious. He was too frightened to mask it.

'Pendelton, you're just diggin' your hole deeper.' Trimble took a step forward, flinging the newspaper back onto the desk, eyes never leaving Clavin.

Clavin's fear got the better of him. He spun, tried to dash from the doorway.

Trimble moved a hell of a lot faster than Clavin thought a man of that size should have been able to. Trimble was still sober, that was the problem. He still had his coordination. He caught the back of Clavin's shirt and jerked him backward. Clavin slammed into the side of the door frame, catching the brunt of the blow on the side of his face. Pain splintered through his cheek and jaw and stars exploded before his vision. Trimble immediately hurtled Clavin forward into the livery proper.

Clavin landed in a heap near a stall, groaning. Trimble clomped after him, reaching down and hoisting him up. He jammed him against a beam, pressing his face close.

'You know, Pendelton, I was right kind to you last time. I gave you another chance but you decided you was too big for yourself. Now I got a problem I rightly don't care to have.'

'I-I'm sorry, I thought, I thought he could help. I was just thinkin' of — '

'You weren't thinkin' of nothin' other than causing me trouble, Pendelton. This is my town. I'm the law here. You damn well know that. Everybody knows that. I want you to think on that real good after you wake up at the doc's with half your bones broken, you goddamn Nancy Boy.'

Trimble jerked back a fist and pounded it into Clavin's face. Blood spurted from his mashed lips and he knew at least three teeth were loose.

Trimble cocked the fist again and Clavin prepared himself for death.

★　★　★

Hannigan watched Trimble move along the boardwalk until he came to an alley that ran beside the livery. Without so much as a look behind him, he slipped into the alley. This was Trimble's town; that was plain by the way he gave no thought to being followed or questioned.

Hannigan waited a few moments to see if Trimble came back out but the lawman didn't materialize.

The manhunter scooted across the street, hoping he could still pick up the lawman's trail. No telling which direction he might have taken once he reached the back of the livery. Still, he had to use caution, in case Trimble had lingered, suspected he was being dogged. If the lawdog caught him following, the tension between them would take a turn for the worse. Right now it was a nebulous thing, and until Trimble gave him a solid reason to escalate it, he saw no point in making it substantial.

He eased his way into the side street, scouting the ground for sign. The dirt had been tramped numerous times, but a larger set of footprints, from a heavier man, indicated Trimble's passage. The trail led around to the back of the livery. Hannigan sidled up to the open double doors, dropping his saddle-bags to the ground, his suspicion climbing up a notch.

He wondered if his earlier assessment that the liveryman's bruises were none of his business had been wrong. Was there bad blood between the liveryman and Trimble? Was Trimble responsible for those bruises?

The sound of a body falling sent a ripple of tension through Hannigan's rangy frame. He pressed up against one of the opened doors, listening intently. A voice came from within, muffled, the words lost.

With a clutched breath, Hannigan peered inside the stable just in time to see Trimble slam a fist into the liveryman's face, whom he had jammed against a beam. The dark suspicion in Hannigan's gut crashed home with that fist. Trimble was brutalizing the man now and likely had in the past. The lawman's fist poised for another blow, one that might kill the smaller man.

Hannigan threw aside caution and stepped into the livery. 'Stop it, Galen!'

His voice crashed out and Trimble jolted, looking over to the manhunter, fury on his face. 'Now!' Hannigan came deeper into the livery, hand itching to go for his gun, but the situation required smoother handling. He couldn't pull his gun on a lawman unless he had no choice.

'What the hell you doing here, Hannigan? You following me?'

Hannigan didn't miss a beat. 'Came to make sure my horse got the proper care. Always check on him in strange towns.'

'That why you came in the back way?' Trimble plainly didn't believe his story.

'Let him go, Galen. You'll kill him if you hit him again.'

The liveryman was dangling in Trimble's grip. His eyelids fluttered as he looked pleadingly at Hannigan, blood running down his mashed face.

'This ain't your town, Hannigan. We do things different here.' Trimble didn't want to back off and didn't cotton to anyone telling him to do so. The defiance was plain on his face and Hannigan had only one card to play before he had to force the man to let the liveryman go.

'I'm askin' on our friendship, Galen. On those times we rode together. Leave that man be.'

Hannigan's gaze locked with Trimble's. The manhunter wasn't sure the lawdog would back down, but after a strained moment he apparently read the threat in Hannigan's stance and wasn't quite ready to test it. He released the liveryman and Pendelton slid down the beam to the floor, moaning.

'Hannigan, I ain't used to being told what to do in my own town.' Trimble lowered his fist, curling and uncurling his fingers.

'Why were you beatin' this man, Galen? What'd he do to deserve this?'

Galen let out a chopped laugh. 'What'd he do? Why don't you ask him, Hannigan? Why don't you ask him how good friends he and my dear departed wife were? Then maybe you'll see it my way.' Trimble's glare flashed a message to the manhunter, one that said you got away with it this once for old time's sake, but don't try getting in the way again.

The marshal glanced a final time at Pendelton, then strode from the livery.

Hannigan pulled a bandanna from his back pocket and, going to the liveryman, knelt. He passed the cloth to the fellow, who accepted it, then dabbed at his mashed nose.

'That true what he said about you and Lessa?' Hannigan helped the man to his feet, leaning him against a post so he wouldn't fall back down.

The liveryman shook, terror in his watery eyes. 'Please, please just leave me be. I can't say nothin', I can't . . . '

'You the one who sent me that newspaper?' Trimble had carried the paper when he disappeared into the alley, but didn't have it when he left. That meant he'd left it here some-where, most likely because he suspected the liveryman of having something to do with sending it.

'He'll come back, Mr Hannigan, if I tell you anything. He'll come back and you won't be here to stop him from killin' me next time. I reckon you think I'm the worst kind of coward, but I don't want that. I thought I could stand up to him but I was just foolin' myself.'

'It's a damn stupid man who ain't scared when there's reason. Suppose you just listen. If what he said about you and his wife is true I reckon you got feelings for her and that's why you sent me that paper. I also reckon you know damn well what men hire me for.'

Tears welled in the liveryman's eyes. He slid back down against the beam, folding in on himself and sobbing. 'I loved her, Mr Hannigan. No matter how wrong it was.'

Hannigan reckoned if he had compare the two men who'd been with Lessa Trimble, he could see which one suffered the most from the loss. It wasn't his place to pass judgment and maybe there were some circumstances that made excuses for sin.

'I aim to find out who killed her whether Trimble likes it or not. You got my word on that. You know anything that might be of use to me you can find me at the hotel.'

The liveryman continued to sob, not looking up. Hannigan left him there, wondering just what the hell kind of man his one-time friend really was.

*　★　*

By the time Galen Trimble reached his office anger had swelled to rage. He slammed the door shut and stood in the dusty light of the deepening afternoon, fury sizzling in his veins, making his head throb.

'Goddammit!' he yelled. What goddamn right did Hannigan have coming in here thinking he could run roughshod over Trimble's duty? What right did he have stopping him from punishing Pendelton the way he deserved to be punished? Christ, if it weren't for how suspicious it would look he'd go right back there and kill that Nancy boy for what'd he'd done. Trimble had known immediately that goddamn coward sent Hannigan that paper. No one else was stupid enough to have pulled such a stunt. So instead of facing him like a man, Pendelton had brought a do-good friend from Trimble's past into a situation where he wasn't goddamn wanted.

'Nooooo!' he yelled, whirling and with a thrust of his arm sweeping the silver coffee pot and tray from the table. The coffee pot bounded from a wall, splashing ink blot-shaped brown liquid that ran in rivulets to the floor.

'I swear, Hannigan, you get in my way again . . . ' The words came through teeth clenched so hard his jaw ached.

This was his town, goddammit, and Hannigan would learn that in spades if he interfered again.

Trimble went to his desk and fell into his chair. Yanking open a drawer, he

4

Tootie managed to check into the hotel, take a birdbath using the porcelain basin, pitcher and towel provided in her room, and change her clothes in just under a halfhour. She wasted no time slipping into a drab gray skirt and matching waist-length jacket, white blouse and highlaced shoes. A cameo adorned a blue velvet choker around her slim neck. She pinned back her black tresses with silver combs. When she inspected her look in the small mirror she carried in her portmanteau, which was open upon the bed, she reckoned she looked the epitome of a frontier school marm. The look would tickle Hannigan no end, she bet, blouse buttoned up to the neck, not a lick of skin showing. He was probably having a nice little laugh over it right this moment, figuring he'd hornswoggled her into a more sedate role for this case. The notion irritated her not a little, but deep down she was forced to agree it was probably the best posture at present. Perhaps if other directions presented themselves she could return the favor.

Maybe you're just getting a bit too used to prancing around half-naked, she told herself. There was something freeing about portraying a bad girl, a woman with the luxury to express her God-given attributes in any way she fancied. Once one got past the modesty issue, of course. But mostly it was just because she knew it got on Hannigan's nerves and made him jealous. A small smile creased her full lips.

Fifteen minutes later, she strode from the hotel into the afternoon sunlight, arching her chin a bit and slipping into the demeanor of an eastern school teacher come West. An indignant flaring of her nostrils and tilt of her chin showed folks she was more than a little huffed at the accommodations, or lack thereof, in this dusty little hole stuck in the middle of nowhere. She was a woman of fine breeding, after all, used to the amenities eastern life provided.

'Why, I declare, they don't even have gaslighting . . . ' she muttered with a put-out tone, making sure her affectations were in order.

With a snobbish prance she crossed the street to the opposite boardwalk, her mahogany eyes narrowing as they noticed Hannigan a bit farther down walking into the livery with another man, whom she instantly singled out as the marshal, tin star glinting. The lawdog carried himself with an air of arrogance, his stride cavalier, shoulders back, chest out like a peacock.

She was careful not to get caught peering in that direction and nodded politely though with superiority to others who passed her on the boardwalk. Reaching the general store, she tugged down the gray coat, then entered.

The place, despite sunlight streaming

through a large window, reminded her of walking into a mine. Dust swirled in shafts of amber light, the floor coated with a layer, and cramped aisles held canned goods and various supplies. A man scuttled up to her, his gaze raking her form with a glint of lust, oblivious to the plainness she'd tried to affect. Her face held a natural beauty that made men trip over their tongues and her slim figure drove even the churchly to impure thoughts. Maybe the school marm disguise was going to be harder to pull off than she thought.

'Can I help you, miss?' The man was scrawny, with a neck like a turkey and hair like a graying rooster. His angular face was as homely as any she'd seen. His tone carried the over-eagerness of a snake-oil salesman.

'Stop panting, sir. It's unbecoming.' She made her tone regal and reproachful.

The man licked his lips and took a slight step backward. 'I assure you, miss, I was doing nothing of the sort. I was merely interested in knowing if you had a list so I could fetch your supplies.'

She placed her hand to her bosom, fingers splayed. 'I do declare, I have witnessed less obsequiousness from a dog begging for a cool drink on a scorching Georgia summer day.' She reckoned her southern belle accent hadn't improved any, but the man didn't appear any too bright.

'Ob-see-what?'

'Oh, never mind,' she said with a fluster, wagging her hand. 'Please, do tell me where I might find a certain Mrs Apperby?'

'You ain't the new school marm, are ya?' The man seemed little affected by her snobbish treatment of him, but men would put up with a lot from a pretty gal if they thought they had a chance of getting in the saddle.

'Well, now, that just depends on whether you have a Mrs Apperby on the premises, does it not?'

'Where?' The man scratched his head.

'In your store!' She stifled an urge to laugh.

He frowned. 'Why didn't you just say so?'

'I am most certain I did.'

'Reckon you must be the new teacher then. You sure talk like you had yourself plenty of schoolin'. Maybe you can teach me some things, too?' The lustful glint strengthened in his blood-shot eyes.

'Horace!' A voice snapped from the corner of an aisle where an older woman had stopped to observe them. Tootie's gaze jumped in that direction. The woman's graying hair was yanked back into a severe bun beneath a kerchief. Her worn dress did little to conceal her over-ripe figure. She clutched a can in each hand and looked ready to hurl one of them at Horace, whom Tootie instantly figured to be her husband.

'What'd I tell you about being too nice to the ladies?' The woman's tone brooked no backtalk.

'Yes, mama,' he muttered and slinked

away, gaze locked to the floor.

'Come back here, deary.' The older woman turned and went back down the aisle.

Tootie followed, suppressing a smile. She reckoned old Horace was going to pay for his little stunt later.

'You are Mrs Apperby, I presume?' asked Tootie, when the older woman stopped beside a small crate and placed the cans on a shelf.

She nodded, slapping her hands together then wiping them on her apron. 'You must forgive the old coot. He don't seem to know he was put out to pasture years ago. He'll know by the time I get done with him tonight, though.' A cruel look glinted in her eyes and Tootie suddenly got a notion just why Horace was looking for greener pastures.

'I am certain he meant no harm, Mrs Apperby. I have that effect on men often.' She made sure just enough arrogance leaked into her voice.

'I'll just bet you do.' A note of spite

laced the older woman's voice. She looked Tootie up and down. 'You're too damn pretty to be a school marm, ain't you?'

'Why, I declare, God was kind to my mama and daddy. I am Pauline Twily, yes.'

'He must have gone on vacation for the rest of us.' Mrs Apperby's tone exchanged spite for jealous disgust.

'I'm sure the Good Lord gave us each our own gifts.'

'Yeah? What'd he give me? A no-good little weasel of a husband who can't keep his wick in his own lamp? Seems to be a downright common occurrence in this town. Maybe your Lord was restin' on the day he made Hollow Pass.'

The jealousy vanished, replaced by bitterness. Tootie sized up the woman quickly. She was disappointed in her life, resentful of others whom she deemed to have a better lot. Tootie wondered what she meant by wandering husbands being a common occurrence in this town, but reckoned it had little to do with the case at hand.

'I didn't notice a church in this town, Mrs Apperby. Perhaps it might help if you had one.' She hoped the righteousness in her voice wasn't over-played.

Mrs Apperby laughed, a braying sound pregnant with mockery. 'Yeah, sure, that would help. Why don't you take that up with the marshal? I'm sure he'd love to oblige your notions on that.'

The older woman was taking a secret delight in something. Tootie saw it in her eyes. Another thing Tootie glimpsed there: Mrs Apperby didn't particularly like her, or maybe she didn't like any woman she considered superior in looks. Whatever the case, she had deliberately taken a swipe at the marshal, too. That gave Tootie an opening.

'Why, I get the distinct impression you do not care for your marshal. I must say, I have heard nothing but good about him. He is something of a hero in this part of the West, is he not?' She hoped her voice sounded sincere enough.

The older woman scoffed, moon face scrunched into deep lines. 'I don't like any man who takes it upon himself to take up with a common barwhore while his poor wife's barely cold in her grave. Why, the very next night he was over to the saloon with Miss January, acting like dear Lessa had been gone for years instead of hours. That's why we have saloon girls and no church, you know. Because the marshal sins with the best of 'em and don't want some preacher making him feel guilty — '

'Ethel!' came a voice from down the aisle. Horace Apperby stood there, broom clutched in two white hands, glaring at his wife. 'You know better'n to put down Marshal Trimble. That man's done great things for this town. You know he wouldn't like it if he heard you talkin' that way.'

'Shut up, Horace,' Mrs Apperby said, fire in her voice. 'You got your tail between your legs where that lawdog's concerned. Always jumping up like you got bit by a rattlesnake every time he comes in here. I ain't afraid of that lawdog like everyone else in this town.'

Horace's face reddened, but he held his tongue and walked away.

'Why would anyone be afraid of the marshal?' Tootie asked.

'Because he owns this town, Missy. You'll find that out soon enough if you stay.'

'I have already accepted the position of school teacher. I have come too far to simply leave now.'

'Suit yourself, but you best take my advice and keep your distance from him. You're his type.'

'His type?' Tootie raised an eyebrow.

Mrs Apperby laughed. 'You ain't wearin' britches.'

Tootie nodded, a frown touching her lips. 'You say his wife passed away?'

'She didn't pass away, she was murdered. Hung up like a scarecrow little ways from the school. I reckon that bastard marshal didn't even go lookin' for her till the next morning. By the time he missed her the crows had done their work. Horrible sight.'

Tootie's stomach pinched. 'Who would do such a thing? I declare, what is the world coming to?'

'Don't know what it's coming to but I know where it's going: Straight to Hell.' She shook her head, her chins jiggling. 'He ain't lifted a finger to find out who done it, neither. Poor woman.'

'That is most disturbing, Mrs Apperby. Perhaps I shall reconsider my stay if such things occur in this town.'

'I figure it won't happen again.'

'Why is that? Surely, anyone mad enough to do something so horrible would not stop?'

'Humph, I reckoned it won't happen again because I think that marshal killed her hisself.'

'Oh, Christ . . . ' came Horace's voice, low, from around the corner. His tone carried a here-we-go-again sound.

'Shut your trap, Horace!' snapped

Mrs Apperby over her shoulder. She looked back to Tootie. 'Horace thinks the marshal will find out I been talkin'.'

'I am sure he worries over your well-being, Mrs Apperby.'

The older woman scoffed. 'Huh, he worries the marshal will string *him* up just to teach me a lesson. Me, I'm willin' to take the risk.' She let an ugly smile flitter onto her face.

'I find it hard to believe a lawman would do such a thing.'

'Especially a lawman with such a heroic reputation, no doubt?'

Tootie nodded. 'Well, yes . . . '

'Don't believe everything you read. He's no angel.'

'But he brought down a gang single-handedly, I was informed . . . '

The older women offered a weak smile. 'Believe what you want. Just remember what I said about avoiding him.'

Tootie nodded, making sure she had the proper amount of gratitude on her face. She didn't care for Mrs Apperby any more than the woman cared for her, but it might benefit her to keep her on her good side. 'When do I start?'

'Start what?'

'At the schoolhouse.'

'Oh, yeah. Come in here bright and early tomorrow morning. I'll get you set up with some supplies you have to take out to the schoolhouse. I'll let you use the buckboard. Reckon then you can take a look around and have the younguns there the day after.'

'Thank you kindly, Mrs Apperby.' She gave a slight curtsey.

'Don't thank me. I ain't doin' you any favors.' With that, Mrs Apperby turned and started lifting cans from the crate and stocking the shelves. Tootie left her to her work and headed for the door. She saw Horace give her a pained look as she left, obviously not at all pleased with his wife running her mouth that way.

Tootie had learned as much as she could have hoped. The town lived in fear of its marshal, despite his heroic reputation, and the man carried on with a woman at the saloon. That second part pleased her all the more because it was going to help her get even with Hannigan for the school marm bit. The marshal had a whore named January and whores liked to talk. If she were going to delve deeper into the marshal's activities that would be the best place to start. Could he be guilty of killing his wife? She aimed to find out.

Affecting her school teacher air as she walked back towards the hotel, she had all she could do not to burst out laughing at the thought of Hannigan's face once he found her in the saloon strutting her God-given gifts.

Oh, Mrs Apperby, thank Heaven for sin and sinners, she thought.

5

Tootie had little trouble wrangling a job at the saloon. The barkeep, a weaselly sort with an eye for beauty and a notion to test out the merchandise, had quickly hired her, making none-too-subtle overtures, which she'd deftly fended off.

This time she had chosen a blond wig done in large loops for the job. With a cherry bodice that accentuated her modest bosom and sleek shoulders, and a skirt that hugged her slim hips, she reckoned she'd outdone herself this time. She'd been forced to apply a bit more make-up to conceal the healing scars on her shoulder and jaw from her mishaps in Miller's Pass. She couldn't risk someone, especially the marshal, connecting her with Pauline Twily, school marm.

Workers from local ranches and townsmen who'd closed up shop for the night crowded the saloon. Durham smoke wafted in blue-white clouds and the heavy aroma of too liberally applied perfume, bad whiskey and stale vomit permeated the room. Clumped sawdust ground beneath her high-laced boots. Raucous laughter and curses punctuated the air. A man with a red armband banged away at a tinkler piano against the left wall. Numerous games of chance occupied patrons — chuck-a-luck, poker, dominoes, faro. A long bar ran nearly the length of the north wall, behind which a gilt-edged mirror hung beside a hutch filled with bottles. Portraits of scantily clad women adorned the place and a stairway led from the back up to rooms where the women plied their trade.

She'd already fended off the advances of two cowboys, and she hoped she'd be able to keep it up for the remainder of her shift. Most men appeared more interested in their games for the time being, but it wouldn't take long before the whiskey went to work on their morals and notions turned towards bedding the whores.

Tootie had surveyed the other women in the place. Only a handful worked the room, most of them not lookers with the exception of an older dark-haired gal in a peek-a-boo blouse and frilly skirt. The girl had softer features, dark, likely half-Indian. Tootie guessed that would be January. If the marshal chose a gal in this place he'd go for the prettiest, and this woman carried an exotic beauty that separated her from the rest of the women. She wore far less makeup than the others, carried herself with a certain air of dignity. Tootie had been secretly observing her movements for the past fifteen minutes. While the other women draped themselves over the shoulders of cowboys exhibiting winning streaks, this girl didn't mingle, merely pretended, much in the same way Tootie did. Tootie bet that was because she was saving herself for someone, and that someone had to be Trimble.

Tootie moved towards the bar, where the other girl was leaning against the counter.

Tootie sidled up to the counter beside the Indian woman, silent for a few seconds while pretending to gaze about the room. 'Things pick up early here, don't they?'

The other girl nodded, remaining silent. Her dark eyes glittered and Tootie thought she caught a sadness to them that seemed to bleed from her soul. She tried to size her up quickly but got conflicting signals and couldn't pinpoint anything. She was usually better at reading folks with minimum information.

'I'm Tootie,' she said. 'I'm new here.'

The girl looked her over, but no jealousy or competition came with her gaze. 'January.'

'Like the month?'

'The coldest month.' Her voice was soft, yet carried a seasoning that usually came from women much older. Tootie re-evaluated January's features now that she was closer. She would have placed her age closer to Hannigan's rather than her own nineteen years, which was edging up there for a whore. Her face showed a strange seriousness, none of the wooden-nickel sincerity doves usually carried.

'Always this way here?'

The Indian girl nodded. 'Town unwinds like a spring come nightfall.'

'There a reason for that?'

'You ask a lot of questions.' The girl's tone held no reproach. It was just a statement of fact.

'Didn't realize I did. Like I said, I'm new. Just trying to figure my way around.'

'I suppose you are.'

Tootie decided she'd try a more direct tactic. This girl wasn't one for small talk and she wasn't going to volunteer anything on her own, the way Mrs Apperby had.

'Heard the marshal here's a hero. You think maybe he'd give me a turn?'

Something flashed across the woman's eyes, but Tootie didn't get the impression it was any sort of possessiveness.

'You'd do well to stay away from him.'

'Why's that? He your property?' She tried to sound defensive, as if she'd been caught trying to hone in on another woman's territory.

The Indian girl didn't miss a beat. 'I've been with him. He favors me. But that isn't why.'

'I don't understand.'

The girl appeared on the verge of saying something but didn't. Her face darkened and Tootie followed the woman's line of sight. A man had entered the saloon, his eyes scanning the sea of faces before settling on January. He started towards them, his tin star glinting with light reflected from the chandelier hanging in the center of the room.

'Evenin', Miss January,' said the marshal.

The girl acknowledged him with a short nod, then went behind the bar and drew a bottle from the hutch. Grabbing a clean glass, she came back around to the front, obviously having gone through the ritual before.

She set the glass and bottle on the counter and gave him a small lifeless smile, then walked to the back of the saloon and drifted up the stairs.

The marshal looked Tootie over, a lusty glint in his eyes. She reckoned she might be in some trouble if he got a hankering for something different tonight.

'You're new here?' He took off his Stetson and set it on the bartop. Sliding onto a stool, he dragged the bottle closer.

'Just started today, sugar.'

'What's your name?'

'Tootie.'

He raised an eyebrow. 'I hope that means what I think it means.'

She gave him a coy smile. 'Haven't had any complaints so far.'

The lust in his eyes strengthened. 'Maybe we'll spend some time together right soon, then. For tonight I already got me an appointment.'

Tootie nodded. 'With January?'

The marshal laughed. 'Now don't

you go getting jealous. There's enough of ol' Galen to go around.'

'I'll just bet there is, honeybun.' A thorn of anger for a woman whom she didn't even know pricked her. The marshal's wife hadn't been dead long and here he was, just the way Mrs Apperby said, taking up with the Indian woman.

'What's wrong?' the marshal asked, pouring whiskey into his glass, then setting the bottle back down.

'What?' Her thoughts must have slipped onto her face.

'You were staring at me funnylike.'

'Reckon I heard when I came in you lost your wife a short spell ago.' She decided to test him a bit, despite her better judgment. Hannigan might be reined in by an old friendship but she planned to make a judgment on this man based on her own intuition.

'That ain't none of your business, girly.' His tone iced over, but he didn't seem especially perturbed. He swallowed the glass of whiskey in one gulp and poured another.

'Not trying to be nosy, sugar. Just wondered why a man like yourself would be in a saloon ridin' another woman so soon after his wife was laid to rest.' Damn, she was letting it get personal. She knew better, but she didn't like the impression she was getting from the lawdog. Any normal man would have been grieving, but no sign of pain or loss showed in his eyes.

'You best stop worryin' about other folks' business 'fore you find yourself accompanying her.' His eyes locked with hers.

Well, nothing subtle about that threat, she reckoned. Her assessment of him zeroed in. A cold sonofabitch, one who liked to control situations, perhaps people, one who cared little for the loss of his wife, perhaps had not loved her at all. Did he mean the threat or was it simply bravado? She leaned towards the former. This simply could not have been the same man Jim Hannigan knew years ago; he'd either become someone else or had concealed a side of himself better than Hannigan thought.

Tootie nodded, the weight of his glare unnerving her more than she cared to admit. He went back to his whiskey, downed another glass, then poured a third. She sidled away from him, knowing that trying to dig any information out of him now was not only useless but potentially dangerous. She would have to work the angles and leave him to Hannigan for the time being.

★   ★   ★

After Jim Hannigan set himself up in his hotel room — a small affair with a brass-framed bed, night table holding a lantern, bureau with a porcelain basin and pitcher, a couple hardbacked chairs and green-striped wallpapering — he spent the next hour running over the day's events in his mind. His misgivings about Galen Trimble had begun to coalesce into something he would have preferred to be wrong about. The man was a hero; he'd single-handedly brought down a vicious gang and had just lost his wife in the most horrible of ways. Yet Hannigan had caught him beating a defenseless liveryman and he had the sinking suspicion had he not intervened Trimble would have killed the man. The man who had sent Hannigan a paper drawing him here to investigate, but had been too afraid to contact him directly.

He didn't like the direction that thought was taking him. Despite the fact they were once friends of a sort, all pretense crumbled with the incident at the livery. Galen clearly didn't want him here poking around. Once Hannigan would have attributed that to Trimble's craving for the spotlight, but now he wasn't so sure.

Trimble can't be involved in his wife's death, Hannigan told himself. True, too many times he had seen wives supposedly killed by an outsider turn out to have been murdered by the husband for a variety of unjustifiable reasons. Where there was passion and love sometimes hate and contempt lived hand in hand. A sad fact, one with which Hannigan had personal experience.

But this was different; it had to be. For no matter how cruel Hannigan had caught Galen being to that liveryman, he couldn't believe the marshal capable of murdering his own wife. He couldn't have been that wrong about the man all those years ago, could he? There had to be another answer. Perhaps Trimble detested her for what she had done with the liveryman, and that accounted for his lack of grief over her death, and his fury with the stable owner.

Whatever the case, the murder smacked of a vendetta, and that indicated Joe Crigger. He was the only one left who knew the details of the case, though certainly enough had seen print in pulp books and newspapers to inspire any number of owlhoots looking to make a name. Seemed like an unlikely scenario for one of that type, though.

Most would try a more direct route.

He'd told himself that a good twenty times already, but a nagging doubt remained and Hannigan didn't like nagging doubts. He had to put aside past associations in favor of cold facts. The best way to do that was to start checking with some of the locals to get a handle on just who Galen Trimble had become since they rode together. If Hannigan had been wrong about him being nothing more than a braggart, he needed a contemporary profile of the man. He reckoned the saloon might be the best place to start.

Waiting until evening, he first stopped by the old cemetery at the edge of town to pay his respects to a woman he'd met only briefly many years back. He couldn't think of any Godly words to say but he made her a promise, to find her killer and see to it she rested in peace, for her sake and for the liveryman's. He noticed Trip Matterly's weathered gravestone a short space away, and straggling memories of the three of them, himself,

Trip and Galen, on a case for the Cattleman's Association, drifted through his mind. He couldn't exactly call them good times, though they weren't bad either. But they were one of the few times a loner named Jim Hannigan even came close to forming the normal friendships and camaraderie most men did.

He now walked towards the saloon, shadows crowding the streets, buttery light from hanging lanterns chasing them with each breeze that teased the flames.

Stepping into the saloon, his belly dropped as his gaze instantly locked on a blonde-haired woman stepping away from a man at the bar. He recognized Tootie even with the wig and couldn't stop a sigh from escaping his lips. Somehow she'd managed to beat him at his game again. He had half a notion to throw her over his knee like an unruly child, but it would do no good and likely get him tarred with words for being fat-headed enough to entertain such a notion.

Right now he had a bigger concern, however. The man she had walked away from was Galen Trimble and by the look on her face the encounter hadn't gone whatever way she'd intended it to go. After the way he'd seen Trimble treat the liveryman, Hannigan didn't like the notion of Tootie somehow getting on the lawdog's bad side. It was up to him to deal with Galen, though of course she'd likely tell him he could take his Peacemaker and stick it into an uncomfortable place if he believed that.

She noticed him standing there and gave him a wink, which annoyed the hell out of him.

He made his way towards the bar, his plan about pumping the 'keep for information rushing out the chute. Pulling out a stool beside the lawdog, he settled onto it. Trimble cast him a look but didn't say anything, returning his attention to his drink. Hannigan saw the man was already a little glassy-eyed.

'Galen . . . ' Hannigan signaled the 'keep for a whiskey, then tossed a silver dollar onto the counter.

'Past is the past, ain't it, Hannigan?' Trimble didn't bother to look at him.

'Reckon I don't catch your meanin'.' He accepted the glass of whiskey from the bartender, who cast a jerky glance at the marshal, a hint of nervousness dancing in his eyes before he walked off. That told Hannigan probably as much as he needed to know about how the folks in this town saw their marshal — that combined with what he'd encountered in the livery earlier. The 'keep also likely wouldn't prove useful as a source if he feared Galen.

'The things we done, the things we wanted to do . . . Some came about, most didn't.' A slight hitch burdened Trimble's voice. Hannigan glanced at the whiskey bottle, which was down a good three drinks. Trimble was halfway to maudlin, he reckoned.

'Same way for everyone, Galen.' Hannigan took a sip of his whiskey, which tasted akin to piss. 'Reckon you and I got enough tragedy in our past for any ten men, but we chose our destinies.'

'Did we?' He looked at Hannigan. 'Or did they chose us?'

'Same thing.' Hannigan shrugged. 'We ride the trails open to us. Just a matter of takin' the right ones.'

'You'da stayed things might have been different, Hannigan. Maybe you shouldn't have never gone off on your own.' The marshal returned to his glass, gulping at the amber liquor.

'Surprises me to hear you say that, Galen. Didn't you tell me you were the one who enjoyed the spotlight?' Hannigan buried the sarcasm he felt, keeping his voice flat. Even had the manhunter accepted their offer, Trimble would still have been the glory hog of the three. But maybe Trip would have lived; maybe Clara would have, too. Was hard to tell how fate would have played out. Maybe different, maybe not.

'I was half sober, Hannigan, that might offend me.'

'Didn't intend it as such.'

Trimble sighed. 'Yeah, yeah, I know you didn't. Just thinkin' foolishness. Just thinkin' maybe some mistakes might have been avoided.'

Was that regret in Trimble's voice? Hannigan wasn't certain.

'What kind of mistakes we talkin' about, Galen. You got something to get off your mind?'

The marshal's face reddened a notch. 'What the hell you askin', Hannigan?' A challenge in his voice told Hannigan any regret of a moment before had turned to indignation with the blink of an eye.

'We'll let it drop, Galen. Just thought maybe you were aiming at something specific.'

The marshal snorted. 'You misread me, Hannigan. I ain't got no sins I need to confess and you ain't the type to be mistaken for a preacher.'

Hannigan stood, leaving his drink on the counter, no desire to choke it down. 'You're different, Galen. You're not the same man I knew.'

Trimble looked at him, a darkness in his eyes. 'You're wrong, Hannigan. I haven't changed. It's you who did. You went soft, but then you always did have that compassionate streak.'

'Nothin' I ever been accused of, Galen.'

'Maybe not, but I saw it then and it's even more plain now. Maybe it's a good thing you did turn Trip and me down. No place for bleeding hearts out here in the West.'

'Think what you want, Galen, but just so we're clear. The folks who hire me don't usually want justice, they want vengeance.'

'No one hired you this time, Hannigan. Go home.' His gaze locked on his glass.

'You're wrong, Galen. Fate hired me. I aim to give it its money's worth.

6

Death can occur in a heartbeat. Life can alter course in the blink of an eye. In an instant a scar can be seared across a soul, never to heal.

The man's fist slammed down, nothing more than a blur in the dancing flame-light cast from a stone fireplace in the sparsely furnished parlor. But the sound it made hitting flesh, the brittle shattering of bone in the woman's cheek, was far too acutely heard and felt. An odor came to a boy's nostrils, one of burning log mixed with gunmetal. Ash and blood, a sickening combination.

The man was unshaven, a devil in the firelight, dressed in a stained red undershirt and trousers that hung too low about his waist. A hole showed in the underwear, where bristles of graying brown hair poked through. Flecks of spittle gathered at the edges of the man's mouth and hell shown in his bloodshot hazel eyes. Each detail of his appearance burned itself indelibly into the little boy's brain. The stuff of nightmares.

A half-empty whiskey bottle sat on a small end table beside the sofa, a silent witness, a damning companion.

The ten-year-old boy stared from the corner of the room, wide-eyed, heart pounding like thunderclaps against his ribs. Emotion swelled in his throat, choking him. He shuddered at the sight he was witnessing, too petrified to move, too terrified to call out, too young to stop what was to come.

Shouts; crashing, blistering things, profaned with drunken words of hate. Slurred words from the man, pitiful begging from the woman.

She stumbled back, dress torn from the man grabbing her a few moments previous in an effort to force her into an act he demanded of her each night, often with cruel and visible results. Her hair glowed auburn with reddish streaks of firelight, her gentle features now fraught with anguish and hatred for the man accusing her of something for which she was not responsible.

The boy saw the blood streaming from her broken nose, saw the tears rushing from her eyes. She nearly went down, only her indomitable strength of will keeping her on her feet. It was probably that strength, that defiance, that resulted in her death, the boy realized, years later. Had she gone down, given in to the man, she would have lived to see another day; she might have lived long enough to watch her son grow to be a man, a different man from the thing of vengeance he had become.

'Goddamn you, Ernest!' the woman yelled, voice shaky. 'You got no right to treat me this way.' She spat at him, infuriating him all the more.

'I got every right! You're my wife, ain't ya? I'll treat you any goddamn way I please. You're my property and I aim to see no man lays an eye on you ever again.'

She shuddered, trying to keep the torn flaps of her dress together, modesty asserting itself, some sort of defense mechanism. 'He wasn't looking at me, I swear. You're just too drunk to realize how much of a fool you're being.'

The man uttered a harsh laugh. 'An' you're just too goddamn stupid to realize you shouldn't talk to me that way, May. Too goddamn stupid to know your place. I know what I saw.'

'You saw nothing but what you wanted to see because you ain't man enough to keep food on the table for this family. You drink away half your pay when you bother to go earn it at all. Jesus knows how many women see the other half.'

'Shut the hell up!' the man screamed, taking a step towards her.

The boy stared, fighting not to loose his bladder and soil his underwear.

The woman took a backward step

with the crash of his voice. 'It's the truth and you know it. That fella wasn't lookin' at me. He was looking at you and wondering what kind of foolish woman would stay with a man who belittled her in front of everyone at a church supper. He was staring at you because you staggered in there half-drunk and took us out when it was the only place we could go to get a decent meal.'

The man glared at her, the words doing nothing but infuriating him. Even the boy could tell that, but the woman had tolerated all she ever would, and had lost all sense of concern for her own welfare.

'You'll goddamn learn you can't speak to me that way, woman!' The man tensed, every muscle in his jaw rippling, fists clenching into bone-white mallets.

Defiance glittered in the woman's eyes. 'I'm leavin', Ernest. I'm takin' Jimmy with me. You try to stop me I'll send the sheriff after you this time, I swear. I took your horseflop in the past but I won't no more. And I'll be damned if I let Jimmy follow your example. The church already said they'd take us in till we could get on our feet again.'

'You can't be serious?' Something in his eyes that even the boy could see from across the room said he would never let this woman walk away, would never let them walk out that door.

'I *am* serious. I should have had the strength to do it a long time ago. You held me with fear while I watched you drink your life, *our* life away. The sheriff already knows to expect me at the edge of the property. I'm not out there fifteen minutes from now he'll come lookin' for me and Jimmy.'

The man stared blankly for a moment, like a child shocked that his puppy had bitten him for pulling on its tail. Then the death swept back into his gaze.

The man placed his face in his hands, for a moment collapsing onto the edge of sofa.

'Please, Ernest, you knew it was coming. Don't make it worse. Let us go.'

The woman had made a mistake. She misjudged his burying his face in his hands for defeat, perhaps even sorrow. The boy saw compassion on her battered face, despite what the man had done to her. But none came to the boy's face, nor to his heart. He had heard the countless nights of shouting and sound of things breaking, had seen his mother's bruised face the next morning, when she assured him she'd run into something in the dark, when she had made excuses for his father's behavior and cruelness. Cruelness that sometimes extended to the boy himself.

The boy wanted to shout at his mother, warn her that this man was about to become a monster unlike any he'd become in the past. It wasn't sorrow in his eyes; it was desperation and simmering rage.

But he couldn't utter a word. He

couldn't speak and he couldn't stop what was to happen.

The man's face lifted from his hands. A peculiar look rode his features, something vacant, something final. 'You ain't leavin' . . . ' A strange calmness bled into his voice that was somehow more frightening than the thunder of his shouts.

'You have no choice, Ernest. You don't let us leave the sheriff will make you.' She folded her arms, lower lip quivering, but stance determined. 'I'm going to wake up Jimmy now if your shoutin' hasn't already.'

'No.' Just one word, but it carried the shock of a shotgun blasting in a silent room.

She shook her head, pity now on her features. She brushed the blood dripping from her nose on a sleeve, and sniffled. 'I'm sorry, Ernest. Truly I am. But it has to be this way.'

His eyes narrowed ever so slightly. 'I said no.'

She peered at him, the truth

suddenly dawning on her because she started to shake her head and fear jumped back into her eyes. 'Ernest, please, the sheriff — '

The man came off the sofa. 'Let him come. By the time he gets here it won't matter. I told you the day I married you I'd never let you leave. I meant it.'

The woman stepped back as he came forward, slowly, inexorably. Her back pressed against the log wall.

The boy's voice came loose then. He screamed, shrill, piercing, pregnant with all the pent-up rage and terror he'd felt night after night. 'Noooo!' He burst forward, small fists clenched and heart pounding in his throat.

The man turned, a stunned expression freezing on his face.

The boy leaped, throwing himself at the man, fists beating, beating, beating, having all the effect of rain hitting stone.

The man roared, fist lashing out, thudding against the boy's forehead. The boy flew backwards, crashing down against the sofa, the room spinning before his vision.

The woman screamed then and threw herself at the man. 'Leave him be, you sonofabitch! Leave him be!'

He hurled her back, slamming her against the wall. Her small body shuddered, but somehow she managed to stay on her feet, though she could no longer offer any resistance.

'I told you, woman, you'd never leave. Till death do us part. That's what we promised. That's the way it's gonna be.'

The boy's vision cleared, just as the man grabbed a poker from the fireplace and hoisted it above his head.

The woman stared in terror, unable to avoid the blow.

The boy tried to force himself up, tried desperately to help, but his legs wouldn't function correctly and he floundered.

The poker came down in a blurred streak. A hideous crunch of bone sounded as it embedded itself into her skull. Fragments of bone and spatters of blood laid a gruesome streak across the log wall.

Her body seemed to hang there a moment, then crumpled. The man raised the poker again, rage completely overwhelming him. He screamed, bringing it down a second time on her already dead body, then raised it for a third blow.

The door burst open. The sheriff had come early, no doubt attracted by the screams. His gun poised in his hand, it took him only an instant to assess the situation. He fired and Ernest Hannigan jolted, lead punching into his back. He half-turned, shock on his face as he looked at the sheriff.

'Jesus, Ernest,' the lawdog muttered. 'What you gone and done?'

'She . . . she had it . . . comin' . . . '

His last words, forever enshrined in the hell of a boy's nightmares. Ernest Hannigan collapsed, dead before he hit the floor.

The boy began to weep, tears streaming down his face as the sheriff rushed over to him and grabbed him up, spiriting him from the scene. Away from the house he was inconsolable. He simply started to scream and didn't stop until his throat bled and his voice deserted him.

* * *

Jim Hannigan sat bolt upright in bed, sweat pouring down his face and chest, heart thudding. The darkness in the room seemed to throb with the after-effects of the nightmare.

'Jesus . . . ' he muttered, putting his face in his hands. Would the damn nightmares ever stop? Would the ghosts ever leave him be? They haunted him in his sleep as in daylight, had made him what he was, and what he was not. Since that day he'd realized nothing his mother had done put her at fault for what happened. His father was simply a cruel man given to bursts of rage and paranoia, all of which worsened with his descent into whiskey hell.

For years he had blamed himself for that night, told himself the countless lies a child does when unable to understand the cruel tricks fate can play. For as many years he convinced himself that's all families did, screamed and fought, and eventually eroded to a point where one left or another murdered. He'd shut his emotions off, all except for the one called vengeance. He swore he'd never allow himself to get close enough to anyone to ever hurt that way again, to risk having so much taken from him.

Until Tootie.

'Jimmy . . . '

The voice was soft, bell-like, and it startled him. His face came from his hands and he wanted to jump from the bed, but his legs refused to work. As if they were filled with lead, he seemed cemented where he was, only able to stare at the glowing apparition standing near the window.

In the darkness of the room, the figure seemed transparent, wavering, auburn hair shimmering with unearthly light. Her features radiated as soft as he recollected, a hint of a smile on her serene face.

'You can't be here . . . ' he whispered.

She didn't turn from the window, merely kept looking out with an oddly placid expression. Her lips didn't move but he heard her voice. 'You were never to blame, Jimmy. Your father . . . he was a cruel man. You could not have stopped him.'

'How . . . how are you here?'

'Perhaps I'm not . . . ' the figure said, lips still holding their smile. She turned to him, then, and he saw the sadness in her eyes, saw a tear wandering down her face. 'Perhaps I am no more than a dream.'

'This can't be real. I don't believe in ghosts.'

'Don't you, Jimmy? You've let them haunt you all these years.'

'I don't understand.' He struggled to move his legs but they remained unresponsive.

'I think you do . . . ' The figure paused, the sadness in her eyes growing. 'There's not much time. I can't stay more than a moment. She loves you, Jimmy. Let her in. It's not the way it was with your father and me.'

'She'll die if I let her in . . . ' His words were a reflex, something he'd thought countless times but never expressed aloud.

'Perhaps. It's risk we all take. But if you don't . . . that man your father was will live in you, in the bitterness you carry.'

'I'll never be like him. I've spent my life making sure of that.'

'Have you? Or have you simply directed his violence into something else? He never loved, Jimmy. He never truly cared about another human being.'

'I can't risk her life.'

Deeper sadness came to the apparition's face. 'Don't let what you felt that night destroy what you could have with her. You have a choice, Jimmy. Your father lost his. Let your fear stop you from living and you'll be the same man your father was. Leave that night behind now. Let her help you.'

He struggled to find words, but his mouth suddenly wouldn't work and emotion choked his throat. The room about him seemed cottony, blurred at the edges. From somewhere in the distance a muffled beating pried at his senses. The figure before him shimmered, swayed.

'Good-bye, Jimmy . . . ' The woman's smile returned, softened.

A thunderous bang rang out and her glowing form splintered into a million glowing, fading fragments. Hannigan blinked, shaking his head.

The room was dark, the vague outlines of the chair in the corner and bureau visible. His legs came free and he swung them out of bed, drawing a stuttering breath, sweat pouring down his chest. All signs of the ghostly figure had vanished, dissolved into nothingness.

Christ, you were still dreaming, Hannigan. You had to be —

Another bang made him start and he realized this time what caused it. Someone was shooting, outside in the street. He managed to get to his feet, shaky, and stumble his way to the window.

The muffled beating he'd heard was the sound of hoofbeats tearing through the street. A rider came charging hard below, an eerie figure completely garbed in black. Some sort of black mask covered his face and a black duster whipped backwards in the wind. From the distance Hannigan could tell little else other than the figure had blasted out a merchant's shop window.

The figure on horseback drew up, the black horse beneath him rearing, hoofs beating the air. It neighed as it slammed down onto all fours and the rider heeled it into a prancing gait that took him left then right. He leveled the gun in his hand, triggering another shot that sent lead punching through another window. The window shattered in an explosion of glass that rained to the boardwalk and floor within the shop. Letting out a whoop, the ghostly figure pumped three more shots into a water trough, which spouted streams.

The rider drew up, reloading, then blasted away at more windows.

Hannigan jumped away from the window. Grabbing his trousers and shirt from a chair, he quickly dressed, then buckled his gunbelt around his waist. After yanking on his boots, he ran for the door.

Coming out into the hall, he saw Tootie, still in her bargirl costume, poised at the door of her room.

'Stay put!' he snapped, hastily locking his door and pocketing the key, then running down the hall. A measure of relief took him when he didn't hear her following, but he had counted on her wanting to maintain her cover unless breaking it couldn't be avoided. He knew she'd be watching from the window in case he needed backup.

He made his way down the steps in leaps, then sprinted across the lobby. Plunging out into the night, he saw the rider down the street, still shooting at various targets, doing as much damage as possible. An instant later, the figure holstered his gun.

Hannigan's belly plunged as the rider reached into a saddle-bag and withdrew a bottle filled with some sort of liquid, a rag stuffed into the top. Reining up, the rider's other hand fished in a pocket of the duster, but Hannigan couldn't see what he took out. An instant later it became clear as a Lucifer flared and the bottle flamed into a firebrand. The rider hurled it, the bottle a yellow-orange streak as it tumbled through the air to explode with a whoosh against the boardwalk.

A man, sleepy-eyed, came from a building and saw the flames. The fellow started yelling at the top of his lungs. The figure drew his gun again and took a shot at him, but the bullet hit so far wide Hannigan knew the figure had missed on purpose. The shot was meant to induce fear, not death. The yelling man's mouth clamped shut and he darted back into his home.

The dark figure, looking backward, saw Hannigan and stiffened. For a dragging moment, the rider froze, gaze locked on the manhunter. Suddenly he whirled his horse around and with a sharp 'Yah!' kicked it into a gallop. The rider came careening back towards Hannigan and for a moment the manhunter thought the figure intended to gun him down. But the rider charged past, raising clouds of dust, never firing a shot nor even giving Hannigan another look.

Hannigan raced towards the saloon, where three horses stood hitched outside to the rail. The mounts likely belonged to cowboys too drunk to ride out.

He grabbed the nearest horse, untethering the reins, then swinging into the saddle. He reined around and heeled the mount into a gallop.

Only moments separated him from the dark rider, whose dust was still settling, leaving a clear trail through town. Hannigan followed, the horse's hoofs eating ground as it picked up speed.

The dust dispersed as the rider reached the hardpacked trail. Darkness seemed to swallow Hannigan at the outskirts of the town. The moon cast a wan light across the countryside, but the forest loomed, nearly pitch black, to either side of the trail.

It dawned on him he'd thrown caution aside and made himself an easy target had the rider wanted to kill him back in town. The notion gave him pause. Joe Crigger wouldn't have missed such an opportunity, would he?

Even now he was being reckless, chasing an unknown shooter into the night. Sloppy and careless, driven by emotion instead of skill. He'd done that far too often lately.

Eyes narrowing, he steeled himself, trying to pick out details on the trail ahead in the pale moonlight.

The figure seemed to have vanished and any dust in the air had settled. Something was wrong, and now that Hannigan was alert he felt it in his very being. He slowed, gaze sweeping back and forth but seeing no signs of the rider. That meant the shooter had stopped.

A shot thundered and Hannigan's horse suddenly staggered in its step. The animal jerked to a skidding halt, neighing in fright. Hannigan fought with the reins as it started to buck. His skills as a horseman far trailed his skills as a manhunter. Muscles in his arms quivered and his hands bleached. The animal danced left, right, kicked backward. He had all he could do to stay in the saddle.

Hannigan had realized his recklessness too late. In the few moments the manhunter had taken his eyes off his quarry, the rider had gone off-trail, prepared for an ambush. A bullet had opened a gory slash across the horse's flank, sending it into a panic. Another shot meant to frighten, not kill, wholly effective.

Had the mount been Hannigan's own, he might have had a chance. His grip was slipping and sweat broke out across his forehead and chest. He struggled to keep his hold on the reins, squeezed his legs into the mount's sides, but it had no effect.

A foot tore from the stirrup. The horse neighed and reared, slammed down. Hannigan canted sideways, losing the reins. Desperately clutching at the horn, his fingers slipped. The mount shot straight up in the air, kicking out, then crashing back to the trail in a bone-jolting impact that lifted Hannigan completely out of the saddle.

The mount was no longer under him. Arms windmilling, he went through the air as if in suspended motion, though his flight took less than a few heart-beats. On instinct, he managed to tuck his legs against his chest and come down in a roll against the hardpack that seemed only slightly less jarring than hitting a stone wall. Sharp branches clawed at his face and pebbles bit into his sides as he tumbled end over end. Coming to a stop in a patch of thick brush, he lay gasping, pain radiating from more areas than he could count, but lucky to be alive. No bones appeared to be broken, but his pride had taken a couple fractures. He struggled to get to his feet, managing to reach hands and knees before a sound came to his ears.

A footfall in the brush, then another. He looked up, his gaze settling on a dark figure outlined against the moon. The rider looked like something from a nightmare, an apparition in a black duster, trousers and shirt. The vague outline of stitching showed on the ebony mask. The man leveled a Smith & Wesson on Hannigan, at first not saying a word. The manhunter knew he had no chance at getting to his feet before a bullet drilled into him.

'This ain't your fight, Hannigan . . .' The figure's voice came low, raspy, an obvious attempt to disguise its real sound. 'Go back to wherever you came from.'

Hannigan caught his breath, wiped sweat from his forehead with the sweep of a forearm. 'I can't do that, Crigger, or whoever the hell you are. You killed an innocent woman.'

The figure didn't answer for a moment. The breeze ruffled his duster, making him look more eerie in the alabaster glaze of moonlight. 'Her death couldn't be helped. She belonged to him. I aim to take every thing he has before I kill him.'

'You murdered her, plain and simple. Whatever your beef with Trimble, you had a choice.'

'He had a choice, years ago. He made the wrong one. Now his debt's come due.' The figure took a step forward. His voice lowered. 'I'm warnin' you, Hannigan. Leave Hollow Pass. You get in my way again and next time I might be forced to kill you.' Without warning the figure kicked Hannigan in the face.

A bootheel collided with the manhunter's chin, stunning him, sending him over onto his back. The copper taste of blood soured his mouth and bursts of light glittered before his eyes.

Through a haze he heard the sound of the figure's steps retreating through the brush, then, a moment later, the clopping of hoofs that quickly faded into the distance. Forcing the cotton from his senses, he pushed himself up, shakily gaining his feet, pain throbbing through his jaw.

He stumbled back onto the trail, gaze searching both directions but seeing no sign of the figure. He'd have no chance of trailing the rider in the dark without a horse and his borrowed mount had bolted back towards town.

Shaking his head, Hannigan started walking back towards Hollow Pass. A surge of disgust with himself flooded his veins. The only way that encounter could have gone worse was if the figure had killed him. He'd let himself get distracted. Again. This couldn't go on.

His luck was due to run out and Tootie couldn't always be there to watch his back.

He glanced backward at the darkened trail, moonlight bleeding across the hardpack in cold slivers. That figure might well have been Joe Crigger. He dressed the way his brothers used to dress and he had as much as told Hannigan he was here to make Trimble pay for past sins. Hannigan has half-tempted to let Trimble deal with his own ghosts. Let the arrogant sonofabitch play the hero again and bring in the final Crigger. If it weren't for an innocent woman's death and the promise he'd made the liveryman . . .

By the time he reached town some of the pain in his jaw and throughout his rangy form had dissipated.

Men roamed the street, now, most of them hauling blankets and buckets. They'd managed to put out the fire before it did any substantial damage, but the acrid scent of charred wood hung in he air.

Outside the saloon, leaning against a rail, Hannigan spotted Trimble. The man was only half-dressed, his chest bare and trousers half on. He swayed, having a hard time keeping his balance.

Hannigan approached him, jumping onto the boardwalk and coming up behind the lawdog. Trimble turned, bleary-eyed as he gazed at the man-hunter.

'Where the hell were you while some fool was shooting up your town?' Hannigan made no attempt to conceal the irritation in his voice.

Trimble's eyes narrowed. His hair was plastered to his forehead and beads of sweat dotted his skin. 'What the hell business is it of yours?' The stench of old whiskey rode Trimble's breath.

'Someone could have gotten killed, Trimble. You're s'posed to be the big hero in this town. Do your job.'

'You're pushin' your luck, Hannigan. I let you get away with it once for old time's sake at the livery. Don't reckon on me being so generous again.'

154

Hannigan's eyes hardened. Under the best of circumstances he had no tolerance for threats, and after his encounter with the dark rider his nerves were stretched thin. 'I just had myself a parlay with the man who killed your wife, Galen. He told me to get out. Told me he was going to take everything from you, too. Reckon he has a damn strong reason to go to such lengths. Anything you might want to tell me 'fore he comes back?'

'Don't know what you think that could be, Hannigan. It's Joe Crigger come back to get his revenge for me killing his brothers. Nothin' else it could be.'

'Reckon that's the most convenient explanation, but I got a notion you have more to atone for than you're letting on.' Hannigan was baiting him, taking advantage of Trimble's obvious condition. If the man were hiding anything the manhunter reckoned now might be the best time to make him slip.

'You got no right talkin' to me that

way, Hannigan. I'm gold in this town, goddamned gold.'

Something in Trimble's tone made Hannigan wonder if he'd hit closer to the mark than he expected. 'I gotta tell ya, Galen, from what I'm seeing you're nothing more than a pathetic waste of a lawman living on past glories. That fella killed your wife. He'll kill you you don't straighten up.'

'You sonofabitch.' Trimble sprang from the rail, fist arcing up in a wild roundhouse. The move was clumsy, the lawdog's legs wobbly.

Hannigan leaned back, avoiding the blow completely, then delivered a sharp uppercut that took the big man clean under the chin. Had Trimble been sober he might have stayed on his feet. The lawdog always had been strong as a mule, a mean and formidable fighter.

Trimble's legs buckled as his head snapped up, then back. He thudded onto the boardwalk on his rear, gazing up with glazed eyes.

'Take some advice from an old

friend, Galen. Do yourself a favor and sober up before that killer comes back. Otherwise he'll make good on his promise.'

Trimble's eyes partially cleared, anger sweeping away some of the fog. 'Don't ever do that again, Hannigan. I swear . . . ' The threat was plain and he meant it. Had Trimble been heeled right then he might have tried to kill Hannigan.

The thought saddened him and he shook his head, frowning. He backed away from the lawman, who sat glaring.

To his right, Hannigan suddenly noticed a woman standing just outside the batwings. A bargirl, she looked to be of mixed blood, Indian of some kind. She glanced at Trimble, then gave Hannigan the briefest of smiles before going back into the saloon.

7

Jim Hannigan returned to his hotel room, a leaden feeling weighing on his soul. He'd muffed a chance to nab the scarecrow killer, managed to piss off Galen Trimble yet again and wasn't entirely certain he wasn't going plumb loco after seeing the ghost of his mother standing in his room earlier. So far, it had been a hell of a night. He wondered if it could get any worse.

Fishing the room key from his pocket, he unlocked his door and stepped inside, closing it behind him. He dropped the key into his pocket and removed his shirt, tossing it over the brass bedpost, which he could barely pick out as a dark ball against the blackness. He sat on the edge of the bed and tugged off his boots, then buried his face in his hands, fighting back a surge of frustration and weariness.

'You gonna tell me what happened?' a woman's voice asked from the darkness and Hannigan nearly came out of his skin.

Head jerking up, he peered at the corner holding one of the hardbacked chairs. Eyes adjusting a bit to the gloom, he saw a woman sitting there.

'Jesus, Tootie, you just scared me out of half my years.'

She giggled. 'Since you're older than me I reckon that isn't such a good thing.'

'That's right clever. How long you been waiting to use that line?'

'Long enough.'

'I locked the door . . . '

'Yes, you did.'

He shook his head. 'Someday you're gonna have to tell me how you get into locked rooms.'

'You've said that before. Today's not the day.' A small laugh came from the corner. She enjoyed taunting him, enjoyed letting him know he wasn't the only one with secrets.

Hannigan frowned in the darkness. 'That fella shooting up the town, he was dressed the same way the Crigger Gang used to, just like the article said.'

'So it was Joe Crigger come back to get revenge on Trimble?'

He nodded without much conviction. 'I reckon that's the logical assumption.'

'There's somethin' you aren't saying. You don't think it's Crigger, do you?'

'I don't know what I think. On the face of it it has to be him. He's the only one who could want revenge on Trimble for what happened back then. It has to be connected to that day he brought the Criggers down, otherwise this killer wouldn't be throwing it in Trimble's face.'

'Maybe it's just some hothead who read about the account and wants to make a name for himself.'

'Maybe, but he could have killed me tonight and didn't. He got the jump on me, twice.' He heard a small gasp from her, sensed her tightening up in the chair. 'He let me go with a warning, told me to tell Trimble he was going to take everything from him first. This fella wants to take Trimble apart in pieces. That isn't the mark of a hothead name-seeker.'

'Who else could it be, then, if not Crigger?'

He shrugged. 'Only other I could think of might be Trip, but he's dead.'

'Thought they were friends?'

'They were, but since it was Trip's sister who got killed by the gang, maybe he somehow blamed Trimble. But it don't matter because Trip's buried in the cemetery at the edge of town. Saw his grave when I went to pay my respects to Lessa Trimble.'

'What you're saying is everything leads back to Joe Crigger.'

He nodded. 'Seems that way, don't it? I'm starting to wonder if I can trust my intuition anymore. I thought all the years on the trail had made it infallible but lately I keep missing the signs or scrambling them. I keep making amateur mistakes.'

'You got more to worry about now . . . ' She said it low but he knew she meant herself.

'I met up with Trimble after I came back from chasing that rider. He was half drunk. Had Crigger wanted him dead tonight Trimble would have made an easy target.'

'When I met him at the saloon tonight, he made it plain any talk about his wife was off limits. He's having an affair with one of the bargirls, too.'

'Dark-haired gal, Indian-looking?'

'Yeah, how'd you know?'

'She was standing outside the saloon, watching me and Trimble. Galen took a swing at me and I put him on his ass. I got the notion she enjoyed seeing him there.'

'Wouldn't be surprised, the way that man comes across. His wife isn't cold in her grave and he's with another woman. Mrs Apperby told me he has been with bargirls all along.'

'Trimble always figured himself a ladies' man. Some things don't change.'

'Some things get worse.'

'No longer a mystery who hired me, either.' Hannigan explained the events at the stable, and Trimble's attitude afterward. 'I wanted to believe the best of him, you know? I hoped I was wrong about the things I was thinking. But he's changed, even from when I knew him those years back. We were barely men, then, no more than eighteen or nineteen. Trip was near twenty, the oldest of us. I thought the years would mellow Galen but what I'm seein' . . . '

'You don't like it,' Tootie finished, standing, the rustle of her skirt reaching his ears as she came towards the bed.

'No, I don't. I swear he would have killed that fella at the livery.'

'You're thinking something else, maybe you don't want to put it into words, maybe you haven't completely focused on it yet.'

He peered up in the dim light bleeding in from the street. 'I . . . '

She stopped before the bed. 'You're wondering if maybe it ain't someone

163

Trimble hired to kill his wife or cover up the fact he did it himself. If this ain't all some big production on his part, right down to hiring an actor to shoot up a few things, make a few useless threats to make him look innocent.'

'I can't believe he'd do that.'

'Maybe he wouldn't, but you've seen such things before.'

'Yeah, I have. Too often. But this fella tonight was no actor. He was damned serious about his threat against Trimble and he admitted to killing Lessa for all intents. Reckon Trimble's in the clear on that point.'

'What about the liveryman, think he knows anything?'

'Not sure. I need to get him to talk to me more about what was going on between him and Galen's wife.'

She reached out in the darkness, her fingers touching his chin, lifting his head. The scent of her perfume reached his nostrils and a shiver went through him. 'Tootie . . . '

'Shhh,' she said, as he came to his

feet before her. He swore he could hear her heart beating gently above the quickening beat of his own and feel the heat from her body. 'When you came in, you sat on the bed and put your face in your hands. There's more than just what happened out there tonight with Trimble and that rider. I heard you call out in your sleep. You screamed a name, May.'

'My mother's . . . ' he said before he could stop himself. Maybe it was guilt, a need to assure her no other woman had entered his dreams, especially after what happened in Miller's Pass, or maybe it had just become too difficult to keep up his defenses.

'That's a better answer than I expected I'd hear,' she admitted, and he could hear the relief in her voice. 'Tell me about her, tell me why you had such pain in your voice when you yelled her name.'

'Tootie . . . I, I can't . . . '

'This is coming to a head, Jim. You know that. After what went on in those other towns, it's time to play your cards.'

He could see the outline of her face in the darkness. Maybe it wouldn't be so goddamn hard to tell her, maybe it was worse holding onto the horror of that day. 'She . . . was killed when I was ten.'

Tootie drew a sharp breath. 'I'm . . . sorry. What happened?'

He shook his head, emotion choking his throat and threatening to flood his eyes with tears. 'No, not now . . . '

'Her death has something to do with the reason . . . ' She let the words trail off.

He nodded, unable to say it. 'Now will you tell me how you get into locked rooms?' His attempt at changing the subject was clumsy, but it was the best he could do.

She leaned closer to him, so close he could feel her breath against his cheek. 'I walk through walls . . . '

He almost laughed, her words siphoning some of the tension from his being.

Then something took over inside, a swelling of emotion he had never felt, entirely uncomfortable yet at the same time like the embrace of an angel. His hand drifted up, fingers featherlight against her cheek. He traced the outlines of her jaw, then wandered down her neck to her bare shoulder. She uttered a small gasp as his fingers traveled to her bodice top, easing it downward to free her breasts in the darkness. His hand cupped her soft flesh, the sensation electric, enough to make his legs weak.

Then she was on her toes and in his arms. His lips pressed to hers, the taste sweeter than anything he'd ever experienced. He'd secretly waited a lifetime for this moment, he reckoned, and it was everything he'd ever wanted it to be. He sighed softly, her bosom heaving in his embrace, her softness unearthing sensations he didn't think possible. In that moment he wanted nothing more than to be a part of her, to take her to his bed and say the hell with Trimble and scarecrow riders and the bastard thing that had set his life on the course it now followed.

She drew back slightly, her lips going to his ear. 'I need a promise, if this is to go any farther tonight.'

'I . . . ' He struggled to find words. 'I don't know if I can give you that . . . I don't know . . . if . . . ' His voice faltered and she stepped back from him then, pulling up her top. He heard her sniffle, knew tears were streaking down her cheek. She went to the door, opening it and pausing.

'Decide soon, Jim. I'll be here for you for a week or forever. It's your choice now. I've made mine.'

Then she was gone. The door softly closed and he stood in the darkness, the biggest fool who ever lived, and the loneliest.

*   *   *

January borrowed a horse from outside the saloon. The man who owned it was slung half over a table in the barroom, passed out for the night, if the emptied rotgut bottle beside his head were any indication. She hoisted her skirt halfway up her sleek legs and kicked the horse into a trot.

The marshal had lumbered away to his homestead just outside of town in the opposite direction from which she took. She was thankful he'd finally sobered enough to walk home; she had begun to think she would never get rid of the dirty buzzard. Each time he touched her gall burned in her throat. She hated every moment she forced herself to be with him. She did it because she had to, not because she enjoyed even a second of his filthy touch. She did it because the man she loved made her do it.

She wished he'd just kill the sonofabitch and be done with it. The damn vendetta had consumed him over the years, turned him into someone she barely recognized anymore. At first he'd been so kind, so thankful. But what happened that day long ago corrupted his compassion and soul. Revenge had replaced her as his mistress.

She hit the trail and rode a bit faster, glancing back, careful to make sure no one followed. Everyone in this God-forsaken town was so fool-assed scared of that no-good lawdog they ran to him whenever someone pissed sideways.

A half mile down, she veered off, guiding the horse onto a small offshoot path barely passable for the animal. Moments later, she drew to a halt, then jumped down from the saddle. Leading the bay to a tree, she tethered it to a branch. It snorted nervously as she made her way through brush, her heart pounding with the anticipation of being with him, despite the fact he hadn't touched her in so long.

A small shack loomed dark against the night. Moonlight barely penetrated the canopy of branches and where it did it didn't help much. A number of times she nearly tripped or twisted an ankle.

Reaching the shack, she could hear

his horse snorting out back. At the door, she tapped the signal they had decided on, then pushed it open. The man had his back to her, his form half in shadow. A single lantern burned low on a rickety table in the corner. She closed the door, waiting for him to turn and acknowledge her, afraid that when he did the shame of her night would show in her eyes and his indifference towards it would show in his.

8

Tootie del Pelado was getting damned sick of not sleeping. As she stood in the morning sunlight streaming through her hotel window fatigue plagued her, one that went beyond the physical effects of too little sleep.

She'd gotten so close, nearly to his bed, but he hadn't been able to go through with it, hadn't been able to make her a simple promise. Was that asking too much? His word assuring her he cared and would not desert her some morning at the end of a case?

He had his secret, one he'd only started to reveal to her. She could wait for that, but she needed something more lasting before she surrendered her innocence.

Dammit, it hurt. She'd seen enough men in her life who took advantage of women, and enough women who manipulated men. She had watched her parents murdered and bore the scars of a turbulent life that at times almost seemed like someone else's. But she hadn't shut herself off the way he had. With a few simple words from him, she was willing to risk being hurt. Why wasn't he willing to do the same?

You have to give him time, she told herself, let him come to it on his own. Something like that couldn't be forced or it would be worth nothing. Last night was a start. Things just got out of hand. It shouldn't have gone that far, but she'd gotten over-eager and wanted it so bad she couldn't stop herself. Not that he was entirely blameless. He'd initiated some of it, after all.

She had always told herself she was strong, a rock of a woman who would never let her heart bleed. But she'd deluded herself. She was coming apart inside. She was trapped on a runaway horse heading straight for a cliff.

A sigh drifting from her lips, she finished changing into the gray skirt and waist jacket. She latched the choker about her neck, fingers drifting over the cameo, one of the few things she had from her mother.

A few minutes later she was crossing the street and walking towards the general store to meet Mrs Apperby. She had little enthusiasm for going through with the school marm routine, but she'd promised to fetch the supplies and bring them to the schoolhouse, so she saw little choice but to keep up the disguise, at least presently. The thought of being stuck trying to teach something to a bunch of children while Hannigan worked the case alone in town made her want to scream in frustration. Not that she didn't want kids of her own someday but a room full of them now seemed akin to getting assigned to purgatory.

A buckboard waited outside the general store and Mrs Apperby came from within the shop, waving, as she spotted Tootie approaching.

'Morning, Miss Twily, it is Miss, isn't

it? I never thought to ask.' The older woman's sour expression seemed embedded into her face, though she was making an attempt at being cheerful.

'I declare, it most certainly is.' Tootie's voice came out almost as sour as the older woman's expression.

Mrs Apperby cocked an eyebrow. 'Now don't you worry, pretty young girl like you will fetch herself a fella someday and settle down. You just got to be patient.'

Tootie let an ironic smile touch her lips. 'I hope you're right, Mrs Apperby. I sincerely hope you're right.'

The old woman nodded. 'Mark my word. Just don't pick one like Horace. And maybe get a bit more sleep. You look like hell warmed over, if you'll pardon my saying so. Now come with me and help fetch your supplies.'

Tootie noticed a number of boxes already in the back of the buckboard. She followed the older woman into the store, where she noticed Horace giving her a wary eye. She saw something behind that look but couldn't even hazard a guess at what it might be.

Mrs Apperby stacked her with an armload of books, then bent and lifted a crate filled with ink bottles, pens and various school supplies. They lugged them out to the buckboard and slid them into the back.

'Now you just take these on out to the schoolhouse and set up the way you like. I'll make sure everyone knows to send the children out tomorrow morning for their first day.'

'Great . . . ' Tootie hoped the lack of enthusiasm didn't show in her voice.

For a moment she thought it had and that Mrs Apperby had taken offense to it. The older woman stiffened, her face going dark. But Tootie realized suddenly the woman was staring past her.

She turned, almost starting, as her gaze locked on the figure of Marshal Trimble standing behind her. She must really have been over-tired, because she'd never even heard him coming.

'Morning, ladies.' He tipped a finger

to his hat. Dark pouches nestled beneath his eyes and his stale breath wafted into her face. His eyelids fluttered as sunlight got beneath his hat and he tugged it down. She reckoned he likely had horses tromping around inside his head.

'What do you want, Marshal?' Mrs Apperby made no attempt to keep the harshness out of her tone.

'Go inside, Mrs Apperby. I reckon I'd like to talk to the new school teacher a bit 'fore she rides off.'

'Why?' Mrs Apperby didn't move.

'That's none of your goddamn business, is it? Now go inside before I get that old man of yours out here to put the reins on you.'

Mrs Apperby's face reddened, but though she said she wasn't afraid of the marshal she apparently wasn't fool-hardy enough to push her luck. She made a sound of disgust and went into the store.

'What can I do for you, Marshal?' Tootie made sure to put the southern belle flavor in her tone.

Trimble looked at her, gaze lingering on the scar along her jaw, an odd expression crossing his face. 'I know you from somewhere?'

A bolt of worry went through her belly. Did he recognize her as the bargirl who had tried to question him last night?

'Why, I sincerely expect, suh, I would remember a strapping fellow such as yourself.' She groaned inwardly, but usually the short way around a man like this was through his inflated self-opinion.

'We've met, I'm sure of it. It'll come to me.'

She certainly hoped it wouldn't. 'Is there a reason you wanted to speak with me, Marshal? I really should be getting these supplies out to the schoolhouse.'

He nodded, licking his lips, blood-shot eyes narrowing to a squint. 'Heard you were askin' around about my wife yesterday when you arrived.'

Tootie suddenly realized what the

look on Horace's face had meant. The little idiot had run straight to the marshal and told him about her conversation with Mrs Apperby yesterday.

'Why, Marshal, it's only natural someone would ask questions when they discover the job they accepted is because the former school marm was murdered in a most terrible manner.'

No emotion came onto his face with the mention of his wife's death. That solidified Tootie's impression the man just didn't care what had happened to his wife. 'Askin' questions that ain't your business isn't healthy in this town, Miss. See to it you keep your concerns confined to learnin' the children.'

She wanted to ask him did all puffed-up braggarts honestly think such dime-store threats had any effect, but thought better of it. Oft-times it was prudent not to poke a coiled rattlesnake.

'Marshal!' A yell came from down the street, before Tootie could answer. Her gaze jumped towards the source of the sound. She saw the young Indian woman, January, running along the boardwalk, a slip of paper in her hand.

'What the devil you doin' here this time of the morning?' Trimble blurted as she stopped before him, though his voice didn't carry the same threatening tone it had for Tootie.

'I got a note, Marshal, was told to give it to you.' The girl was out of breath, her eyes wide, a hint of fear in them. She held out the folded piece of paper.

The marshal cocked an eyebrow and grabbed the slip. Tootie angled herself as inconspicuously as possible so she could get a glimpse of the note when he opened it. She got a good look because it contained only five words, scrawled in bad handwriting obviously meant to be disguised. The note read: 'I know what you did . . . '

'Christ!' Trimble said under his breath, crumpling the note and jamming it into a pocket. 'Where the hell'd you get this?'

January's eyes darted and her brow pinched. 'A-a man, he came to my room after you left last night. He was in there when I went upstairs. He grabbed me and threw me on the bed, held a gun on me. He gave me this note, told me I was to deliver it to you and tell you he'd be coming for you soon enough.'

'What'd this sonofabitch look like?' He grabbed the girl by the arms, fingers gouging in deep enough to bring a look of pain to her face.

'It, it was dark, but I could see he had black hair, was tall, I think, with a scar running along one side of his face.'

The marshal released her, face paling a bit. 'Joe Crigger . . . ' Tootie heard him mutter and her own stomach dropped.

'Who?' asked the bargirl, her face now fraught with concern that Tootie got the sudden notion was false. She hadn't seen them interact last night, but for a woman who supposedly was his mistress she seemed strangely detached.

Tootie reckoned that wasn't anything unusual for a saloon girl; the men they bedded were simply a job to them. But she wondered if there were more to it because she caught the slightest gleam of deceit in January's eyes. She made up her mind she was going to try to get closer to this girl, question her deeper.

'Just a goddamn nobody,' the marshal said.

'Trimble!' A man's voice crashed out in the warm morning and the lawdog spun. Tootie's gaze jumped to a figure stumbling out of the livery. The smallish man looked a wreck, his shirt hanging from his trousers, his hair matted and face a bruised map. An insanity showed on his face, murder in his eyes. He held a Smith & Wesson at arm's length, its barrel aimed at the marshal.

Tootie stiffened and her heart jumped into her throat. It took no leap to figure out who the man was and what he had in mind.

'What the goddamn hell do you think you're doing, Pendelton?' He winced as he yelled, the thunder of his own voice obviously making his head bang.

'You killed her, you sonofabitch,' the liveryman yelled back. 'I know you did!' Folks on the street stopped in their tracks, pulling back to the sides as they saw the man aiming the gun at the lawdog. Tootie swore she caught a certain measure of hope on a number of the faces. They'd be just as pleased to see Trimble meet his maker.

'You're drunk, Pendelton. Go sleep it off 'fore I decide not to be so charitable.'

The man laughed, a sound utterly devoid of reason. He was a tortured soul; Tootie could see it. Hannigan had said this was the man who brought them here, a man who cared for Trimble's wife and wanted justice for her. Apparently he'd gotten tired of waiting for it and was taking matters into his own hands, without a shred of rational thought. His hand shook and the gun jittered. He had no experience with the weapon, that was plain, but a nervous man made mistakes, was more likely to pull the trigger by accident before he could be talked down.

'You want me to tell the good folks of Hollow Pass about your wife, Trimble?' Pain bled into Pendelton's voice, making it waver.

Trimble's eyes narrowed. 'Goddammit, Pendelton, I swear — '

'Don't!' snapped the man, motioning with the gun. Trimble froze, hand itching to go for the gun at his waist. 'Let me tell y'all just what kind of man your hero marshal is. You see that woman there.' He ducked his chin at January, who started. 'She's his whore, but you all knew that, didn't you? Seen him with her plenty of times but you're all just too damn afraid to say so. I was scared, too. I was a goddamn coward because he beat the hell out of me, threatened me, and I let him. But his wife, he beat her worse, beat her until she ran to my arms. I loved her, Trimble, you goddamn sonofabitch. I loved her and she loved me. She was going to leave with me right before you killed her.'

'Christ, Pendelton, you just put a nail in your coffin for that.'

'Admit it, Marshal, you killed her. Tell them!' The last became a frantic yell and Tootie felt sweat trickle down between her breasts. She saw no way out. Someone was going to get dead unless she did something.

'Why don't we just talk this out,' she said to the liveryman, using a soothing voice, trying to calm him. 'There's no need for anyone to get hurt.'

He glanced at her. 'Who are you?'

'I'm Pauline, the new school teacher. Please, this will only lead to no good. Why don't you put the gun down and — '

'No!' The man's hand jittered harder. A slight twitch and he would pull the trigger, send a bullet crashing through Trimble's chest.

Trimble saw it and some of the color left his face, but, seizing on the man's momentary distraction, his hand was already in motion, grabbing for the gun at his hip.

★ ★ ★

Jim Hannigan wasn't getting much shuteye lately, either. He'd been leery of trying after the nightmare anyway, but the incident with Tootie had sealed the deal. He'd spent the remainder of the night staring up at a speckled ceiling. The feel of her skin and scent of her body kept stealing into his mind; the taste of her kiss lingered in his thoughts. He'd never felt anything like it, never felt so completely taken away from who and where he was.

She had asked for a simple promise and he had been too mule-headed to give it to her. He had wanted to, maybe needed to, yet just hadn't been able to get it out.

You're a bastard, he assured himself for not the first time, nor the last.

She was right: the choice was his. A week or a lifetime. He knew which one he wanted, but could he let himself have it? Could he risk her life more than he had already? Did love mean more than violence and loss?

He splashed lukewarm water from the basin into his face, then dried off, tossing the bunched towel onto a chair and shaking his head. He gazed at his haggard reflection in the mirror tacked to the wall over the bureau. Christ, he looked like hell. His face appeared years older suddenly, the dark half-circles beneath his hazel eyes almost livid, the lines about his mouth and on his brow deeper.

You're making this a lot harder than it has to be, Hannigan. Tell her . . .

Tell her what? That he wanted her to stay? That he damn well might be in love with her? Christ, did he even have any idea what love was after all he'd seen occur between his folks?

Telling yourself you would be putting her life in danger is just an excuse, Hannigan. You're just scared.

He let out a clipped laugh. As he had

told the liveryman, it's a damn stupid man who ain't scared when there's a reason. And that reason was a woman who meant the difference between life and mere existence.

Going to the bed, he pulled on his shirt, then strapped his gunbelt to his waist.

The sun had climbed over the horizon by the time he reached the street, splashing the world with honey and gold. A glance took in the shattered windows and burnt patch of boardwalk from the previous night's marauding. Not an inordinate amount of damage, merely a message delivered to Trimble, one that said, 'I'm taking this town from you, then I'm taking your life and no force on earth can do a damn thing about it.'

Hannigan stopped at the cafe and downed nearly an entire pot of Arbuckle's. He couldn't force down any food, but the coffee cleared some of the cobwebs from his brain.

After, he went to the telegraph office,

which was already open for business. He decided not to rely on the operator, in case the man got the notion not to send the message and run straight to Trimble with it. Hannigan didn't know how many were in the marshal's pocket, but better to err on the side of caution.

He insisted on tapping out the message himself, and the operator relented after a clipped discussion and the exchange of a gold eagle. Apparently loyalty in this town only went so far.

Hannigan requested any present information on the whereabouts of Joe Crigger from his Pinkerton friend, and asked him to put legs on it. He told the operator he'd be back to collect the information later and it best not be seen by other eyes first.

Leaving the telegraph office, his mind wandered back and forth from what had happened with Tootie last night to the suspicions plaguing him that Trimble was somehow more deeply involved in this case than he let on. But how? And why? If indeed Joe Crigger had returned to seek revenge, why wait so many years? Had he figured that after all this time he was free to sneak back into the country and retire the marshal permanently? Some outlaws held grudges, as Jim knew only too well from his previous case, but since Trimble single-handedly brought down the gang, would Crigger risk going up against him alone? Taunting him first? It appeared suicide on the face of it. Why warn Trimble when a single bullet fired from a hidden location would have done the job?

Something about the whole situation wasn't fitting together neatly in Hannigan's estimation, but he couldn't figure out what.

The thoughts froze in his mind as he heard raised voices coming from ahead. His gaze jumped to the street a few blocks down. He saw the liveryman aiming a gun at Trimble, who stood on the boardwalk, Tootie and the girl from the saloon last night standing nearby.

'Oh, Christ, no,' he muttered, a white-hot poker of dread skewering his belly. That fool liveryman was going to get himself killed. He was no match for a seasoned lawdog like Trimble. Hannigan had promised him he'd find Lessa's killer, why hadn't he waited?

Hannigan hurried forward, hoping to stop things before they went too far. He had no idea how long the standoff had been in progress, but it was obvious things had reached a critical point.

Ice filled his belly. He saw the liveryman's gun waver just an instant, then Trimble's hand sweep towards the Peacemaker at his hip.

Trimble was still goddamn fast. That was something Hannigan had always ceded to him, probably the one thing not a part of the lawdog's bravado. The manhunter was contained lightning himself, but with Trimble speed had been a God-given gift. Alcohol had likely shaved a hair off his timing and coordination but not enough to save the life of the liveryman.

'Nooo!' Hannigan shouted, his voice seemingly suspended in time and air.

Trimble's gun whipped up. The blast roared like caged thunder in the early-morning stillness.

Blue-white smoke wafted up and Trimble's face flashed a vicious, satisfied expression.

The liveryman jerked, then went stiff, seeming to freeze where he stood. An instant later, he crumpled, the gun dropping from his fingers and his body hitting the rutted street in a spasming heap.

Hannigan ran to him, dropped to his knees, at the same time flashing a glance at Trimble. 'Put your goddamn gun away!' he yelled. Trimble smiled, but slowly lowered his Colt and slid it into the holster.

'Why the hell you'd go and do such a damn fool thing?' Hannigan asked the liveryman.

He was dying. No way around it. The bullet had drilled straight into his thin chest and blood pumped like a well gushing. The man's lips trembled, trying to form words. 'I . . . I wasn't a coward, Hannigan. Not . . . not this time . . . I wouldn't have hurt him . . . I just . . . wanted him to admit . . . to admit . . . he killed . . . ' Any further words died with the liveryman. The fellow's head fell back and Hannigan ran his fingers over the man's eyes, closing his lids.

Coming to his feet, he peered at Trimble who had come up beside him and was looking down at Pendelton. Tootie and the bargirl, their faces drawn, came up behind them.

'You didn't have to do that, Galen . . . ' Hannigan said, voice cold.

'No?' Trimble cocked an eyebrow, arrogance on his face. 'He drew on me, was going to kill me. I had no choice. No one'll miss the little bastard.' Trimble laughed, gave the body a kick, then turned to the bargirl. 'Come on, time for breakfast.' He wrapped an arm harshly about her shoulders and pulled her with him. Hannigan saw a disgusted look flash across her face, quickly hidden. Her dark eyes met his as they walked away and he wondered just what lay behind the look.

He glanced at Tootie, who closed her eyes a moment, then looked at the ground, face painted in the colors of sadness. The death of an innocent man was something they would never get used to. The man lying in the street only wanted justice for a woman he loved; instead he'd gone to join her. Hannigan hoped there was some small consolation somewhere in that thought.

9

Moonlight glazed the dark hulk of the ranchhouse a hundred yards distant. Its generous lines boasted an owner who lived a life of means. The frame house contained at least twenty rooms, was of Greek Revival style with columned porches and thin board siding painted white. Eastlake-style latticework, cut-outs and rows of spindles and knobs accented the building. The roof was steeply pitched, gabled. Double-hung sash windows held twelve panes of glass and sported arched tops. A handful of outbuildings peppered the landscape and a large stable stood to the left of the mansion.

'So that's what a fool's gold buys you,' said the dark figure on horseback poised at the edge of property. The figure tensed, fury sizzling in his veins for the man who owned such an extravagance while the people in Hollow Pass existed in modest dwellings, like serfs to their king. 'You always were the one everybody had to pay tribute to, weren't you, Galen?' The figure's voice came raspy with hatred. 'You took what others had and didn't give a damn about the consequences. Made a goddamn spectacle of yourself for the whole world. I wonder how they'll write about your death after they find out what you did . . . '

The figure, garbed in black, gigged his black horse into a trot. Circling right, he angled around an ice shack and headed for the house. The moon glowed like the Devil's eye, free of the wispy clouds that muted its glow on the previous night, as if it looked upon the task that lay before him and condoned it.

'By the light of the moon, by the light of a star, let me stab at thy cold black heart . . . ' the rider whispered, as he approached the right side of the main house and slowed. A light burned in one of the windows. Good, he was still up. Wouldn't do to have him die quite this soon. Better to let him watch his precious castle crumble to ruin, another piece of his life torn away.

The figure drew up, hand going to his saddle-bags and lifting the flap. Using caution, he lifted out the first bottle, which was filled with kerosene and stuffed with a cloth wick. He fished a Lucifer from his pocket and snapped it to light against the saddle. He stared at the glow, flames dancing in his eyes through the holes cut into the scarecrow mask that concealed his features. A small laugh came from his lips.

'Will you remember this, Galen?' he asked, voice ghostly in the moonlit night. 'Will you recollect this is how you took down the Criggers?'

The figure touched the match to the cloth, then jerked back his arm and hurled the firebrand. It sailed upward, smashing against the roof with a *woof!* Flames whisked across dry wood. With no rain for the past two weeks and warm days, the house made perfect kindling.

Reaching into the saddle-bags a second time, the rider drew out another bottle. He skritched another match to light and touched the makeshift wick. With a quick snap of his arm the bottle sailed through the air and exploded against the long porch. Flames zipped across the boards.

Another bottle came from the pouch, the last one. That would be enough. The figure lit the firebomb and hurled it at the far corner of the house. It crashed against the siding, wall catching instantly.

Commotion came from within the dwelling. The rider smiled beneath the stitched mouth of the mask. For a moment he had thought the stupid bastard had passed out drunk and would perish with the home. The door flew open and a man staggered out, with a dazed look peering about at the flames eating the porch and sizzling from the roof and side of the building.

A guttural curse tore from his throat and he wavered. Drunk, at least halfways, but the gravity of the situation penetrated his sotted brain. The rider laughed, satisfaction flooding him like laudanum.

Galen Trimble's hands pressed to the sides of his head as if he were trying to deny the roaring crackle of flames in his ears.

'Galen!' the rider yelled, keeping his voice raspy. No need to have the sonofabitch recognize him at this point. No, that he planned to save for another time, when they met face to face and Galen Trimble looked into the eyes of the man who would end his life.

Trimble's hands came from his head and his gaze sought to focus on the dark figure. 'Christ . . . Crigger?' he yelled, taking a step.

'Advise you to get the hell off the porch unless you want to burn with your house.'

'Why are you doing this to me, Crigger?' shouted Galen, stumbling down the porch steps, clutching at the rail so he wouldn't tumble down. 'Why did you come back?'

'Old debts need paying, you sonofabitch. This what you bought with Crigger gold?' The figure ducked his chin at the house. 'Was it worth it?'

Trimble reached the bottom of the steps. Had he remained a moment longer he wouldn't have made it off. The house had become an inferno. Flames covered the entire side now, enveloped most of the roof. A great wavering glow painted the landscape in blood and amber. Huge plumes of smoke swirled upward into the night.

The flames highlighted Trimble's reddened face. Fury burned in his eyes. The rider saw the lawdog's hand start toward the gun in the holster at his waist.

'Don't!' the rider snapped, hand sweeping down to jerk a Winchester free from the saddleboot. One smooth motion and the rifle was up and aimed. The rider had accounted for such a move from Trimble, knew his speed on the draw. He levered a shell into the chamber just as Trimble's hand reached his Peacemaker and started it on its upward course. The lawdog's reaction time was pitifully slow. Whiskey had seen to that.

A shot blasted from the Winchester. Trimble's hand jumped and the Peacemaker flew from his grip to land a handful of feet away. Blood streamed down his hand.

'Go for it again, Trimble,' said the rider. 'I'd prefer to wait until you have nothing left, but I'd oblige your death right now if that's the way you prefer it.'

Trimble clutched at his wounded hand and glared at the demon on horseback. 'I'll kill you, you sonofabitch.'

The rider laughed, flipped the Winchester back into the boot. 'Still the braggart, I see.' Reining around, he sent the horse galloping off into the night, leaving Trimble shouting a curse behind him.

He guided the animal along the trail, suddenly pulling it to a stop, then reversing direction and riding into an offshoot path snaking through the woods. The going became laborious, even treacherous, but he wanted to see what came next, needed to savor his victory. Fifty feet farther on he dismounted, tethering the mount to a branch, then continued on foot. He reached the edge of the property, concealed himself behind the thick bole of a cottonwood. The distance was farther than he would have liked, but he could still see Trimble. The lawdog had collapsed to his knees and was screaming in rage. Again the smile came beneath the mask.

The sounds of hoofbeats reached his ear, barely heard above the roar of flames reaching to the sky now. Riders from town, no doubt drawn by the glow.

They came fast, drawing up and jumping from their mounts. A handful of them, running to troughs after grabbing any bucket they could locate in the stable. But their task proved monumental and futile.

With a thunderous boom, a beam snapped and part of the house collapsed. Great clouds of smoke and snapping showers of sparks signed the night. Ash geysered, falling back like gray snow on the man making a sad spectacle of himself, now wailing into the earth. More beams buckled, each taking down another portion of the Trimble castle. By morning, nothing would be left but a mocking testimony to stolen gains and spilled blood.

Another rider came along the trail, outlined by flame light. The dark rider tensed, uttering a curse. 'Hannigan, I told you to get the hell out. This ain't your fight.'

Hannigan. Manhunter. Like a dog on a bone once he got a taste. But dangerous, more so because he held up the truth, didn't waver, the way Trimble had. He wondered what Hannigan would think if he knew what the man on the ground had done.

Maybe that worked into the plan well enough. Maybe it was good the manhunter was here to witness the demise of a western legend.

January had seen Hannigan go into the hotel, had filched the room number out of the clerk, who liked Indian women almost as much as that no-good marshal. Maybe he could use that to his advantage. It was a risk, but he'd gotten the jump on the manhunter easy enough the first time. His reputation was likely as overblown as Trimble's.

The rider eased back into the woods, returning to his horse, then leading it back to the trail on foot. Before mounting, he made sure no one else had gotten curious enough to come running to the marshal's place, but the path was deserted. Most folks likely hoped the lawman was burning along with his home.

He heeled the black horse towards the town. His work for this night wasn't finished. All right, since Hannigan had been foolish enough to ignore his warning, the manhunter was going to help him with Trimble, whether he liked it or not.

★ ★ ★

Hannigan had gotten virtually nowhere since the liveryman's death. He had seen to it the fellow got a decent burial, but that was the best he could do. As much as it galled him, Trimble was well in his rights killing the stable owner. The man had leveled a gun on him, threatened to kill him. The intent to fire or not mattered little. It wasn't something a lawman was required to stop to figure out in the face of danger.

But Hannigan knew Trimble had wanted that man dead and had delighted in the opportunity to accomplish the deed above board. The liveryman's only mistake had been a sudden burst of foolish courage in seeking justice for the woman he loved.

'What are you hiding, Galen?' Hannigan asked himself in a low voice, staring out his hotel room window at the darkened street. 'Is there more to this than Joe Crigger wanting revenge?'

Tootie had told Hannigan about the note the bargirl had delivered and the description she had given of the man who had sneaked into her room. The description fit Joe Crigger; Trimble had said as much.

What did the words on the note mean? 'I know what you did . . . ' Was Crigger looking to ruin and kill Trimble for more than just the death of his brothers? Had something else happened the day Trimble brought down the gang, something that didn't appear in the accounts of the story? Trimble was solely responsible for those accounts, excepting any bit of writer's imagination that might have crept into the pulp novel tales. He might have purposely left something out. But what could be more important to Joe Crigger than avenging the death of his clan?

Things weren't making sense, and with as little sleep as Hannigan had gotten since coming to Hollow Pass his head pounded just thinking on them. He'd spent much of the day scouring the woods where the rider attacked him, finding no trail to the killer in the daylight. Tootie had reported no luck at the saloon tonight, either, as she was unable to corner January because the marshal had corralled her for the entire evening before riding off for home. Tootie had related the report in terse sentences before going to her room, hurt still plain in her eyes. He couldn't blame her.

A noise from the street pulled him from his thoughts. He saw men rushing from the saloon and a couple other buildings, yelling about something, pointing, then scrambling for their horses. Hannigan raised the window and stuck his head out. He spotted a glow in the distance, the occasional flash of flame shooting up like golden claws.

'Hey!' he yelled at one of the men, who looked up. 'What's burning?'

'Marshal's home, looks like,' the man

yelled back, then ran for his horse.

Hannigan closed the window, then went for his door. He stepped out into the hall, glanced at Tootie's door as he locked his own. She was likely asleep by now and he wouldn't wake her. Nothing she could do anyway and risking her identity at this point wasn't prudent.

He ran down the hall, took the steps in bounds, then crossed the lobby. He saw no sign of the hotel clerk.

Stepping out into the night Hannigan went to the livery. He banged on the doors until a smallish man who'd been assigned by the marshal as a temporary attendant came to the door, sleep in his eyes.

'What you want?' the man asked, tone belligerent.

'Need my horse. Marshal's house is burning.'

That got the attendant's attention. It brought a sharp laugh, which the man quickly thought better of and silenced. He let Hannigan fetch his horse. Within a short time, the manhunter had the roan saddled and was heading down the trail towards the burning homestead.

Reaching the grounds, he slowed, seeing men scrambling about with buckets, tossing water into the flames with absolutely no affect. The house was lost, its frame a charred skeleton in places now, most of it collapsed into a burning pile of tinder.

Hannigan heard screaming and looked over to see Trimble on the ground, his face against the grass, a fist pounding the earth. He guided his horse towards the man, stopping before him and climbing from the saddle.

'Galen . . . ' he said, but the marshal didn't acknowledge him. He raised his voice, calling the man's name again.

This time the lawdog looked up, dirt smudged on his face, along with a fury the likes of which Hannigan had seldom seen on any man. His former friend might have been insane for all he could tell.

'What the hell are you doing here,

Hannigan?' Trimble shouted, trying to climb to his feet but falling back to his knees. 'Come to gloat?'

Hannigan shook his head. 'I saw the flames from town. Came to see if I could help.'

'I told you I don't need your help, Mr famous manhunter. I meant it.'

Hannigan nodded, glancing at the flaming remains of the house. 'Who did this?'

'Who the hell you think? That goddamned Crigger.'

'You sure it was him?'

'Hell, yes, I'm sure. I saw him. He was plain as day.'

'You saw his face?'

'He was wearing that goddamn scarecrow mask, the ones the Criggers used to wear.'

Hannigan noticed the marshal's hand bleeding. 'What happened?'

'He shot me, the bastard did. I went for my gun but he had a rifle and shot me when I went to draw.'

'You best get to the doc and have him

fix it up. We can try to pick up his trail in the morning.'

'The hell! There's no we in this, Hannigan. I'll find him and I'll kill him. Joe Crigger's mine.'

Hannigan shrugged. 'I reckon it don't matter who gets him long as someone does.'

'It matters!' Trimble's voice raised to a screech. 'It goddamn matters! He's mine, you sonofabitch. He's mine! I'll have the recognition I deserve for bringing down that *whole* gang. You stay the hell out of it.'

Hannigan stared at the man, seeing no point in arguing with him further. He was too worked up, and Hannigan reckoned he couldn't really blame him after seeing his house turned into ash. Trimble was quickly becoming a man without possessions and without dignity. Or maybe he had lost the latter years ago.

Turning, Hannigan went back to his horse. Without looking back to Trimble again, he mounted and gigged the animal into a ground-eating gait for town.

It took him roughly a half hour to get his roan settled into a stall and himself back to the hotel. Weariness settled over his rangy frame and the vision of Trimble on the ground kept invading his mind. Whatever Trimble was now, Hannigan remembered the time he had been an arrogant braggart, but still possessed a certain pride. Maybe his craving for leaving his mark on history had worn him away, reduced him to the shattered lawman Hannigan had seen tonight. Maybe some other deed had eroded the man he once was, or might have been. Whatever the case, Hannigan felt sorry for him, though he knew the last thing Trimble would want was his pity.

Hannigan climbed the stairs and went down the hall to his room. Pulling the key from his pocket he went to unlock the door, but found the handle turned when he grasped it. He dropped the key back into his pocket, sighing, wondering just how the devil Tootie had managed to get into the room again. She must not have been sleeping after all and seen him ride out. She'd likely want a full report and probably would give him hell for not taking her with him, despite the risk of compromising her identity.

He opened the door and stepped into the room.

'Toot — ' he started but something pressed against the back of his neck. A chill slithered down his spine. He knew only too well what the object was. A gun barrel.

'Step inside all the way and don't turn around.' The voice came disguised, raspy, the same that had come from his attacker in the woods the night before.

Hannigan obliged, getting ready to drop and swing around, in an attempt to disarm the killer.

He never got the chance. The gunbarrel jerked away from his neck but the gate suddenly clacked against his skull, just behind his ear. Stars exploded before his eyes. Staggering, he dropped to his hands and knees. The attacker pushed the door shut, though it didn't close completely. A boot suddenly stomped into Hannigan's back and he let out a grunt, hitting the floor face first.

He saw only blackness before him, spinning blackness.

'Thought I told you to leave town, manhunter?' The attacker put more weight on the boot jammed against Hannigan's back.

'Some folks tell me I'm hard of hearin' . . . ' His vision stopped dancing but he could only pick out the dim outline of the wallboard before him.

'The only reason I ain't killing you now is because I know he hates you. Was always jealous of the man you were. I figure you're going to do me a favor, contribute to the cause.'

'What cause is that?' Hannigan said.

'Reckon I made that plain last night. I took his wife, now I've taken his house. Next time I'll take his sorry life.

He'll pay for his sins.'

'You referring to him killin' your brothers?'

The figure laughed. 'You ain't half the manhunter those books claim you are, you know that, Hannigan? Always figured if anyone would live up to his reputation it'd be you, but I was wrong.'

'You gonna stop talking in riddles and tell me what the hell you're gettin' at? You're jawin' on as much as Trimble ever did.'

'I got a measure of respect for you still, Hannigan, but stay the hell out of my way when I come for him. That make it clear enough?'

'I ain't good with promises, Crigger. Folks would tell you that, too.'

The figure laughed, a ghostly sound in the darkness. 'When you see that sonofabitch tomorrow, ask him some-thin', ask him about Crigger gold.'

'Gold?'

'Didn't you hear the rumors? A fortune in gold and loot came from

Crigger robberies. Never got found, did it?'

'Folks always assumed you took it to Mexico with you.'

'Folks assumed wrong. Ask Trimble. Not that he won't lie about it — '

The door burst open and Hannigan felt the pressure on his back lighten a little.

'Drop it!' A voice came from the door and he managed to twist his head to see a woman in a nightgown standing on the threshold. Her arms were straight out, a derringer in her hands.

The figure in black swore and whirled, his own gun jolting aside the derringer. The small gun fired, the blast exaggerated in the confines of the room. The bullet lodged harmlessly in a wall.

The figure moved, foot coming off the manhunter's back. In a flurry of motion, the figure grappled with Tootie. She kicked at the attacker's shin, bringing bleats of pain, and tried to get the derringer back around and fire into his face.

Hannigan pushed himself up, still shaky from the blow but worry over Tootie drove strength into his legs and arms.

The figure managed to whirl Tootie around, send her hurtling into Hannigan as he came to his feet. They both went sideways, falling onto the bed in a tangle of limbs.

Tootie managed to free herself and get to her feet first, Hannigan still slightly whoozy. She ran to the door and he wanted to yell at her not to make a target of herself but it was too late. She rushed her shot as the derringer came up in the same move that brought her head around the corner of the jamb.

The bullet missed the fleeing figure in black and a second shot crashed out, this time from the attacker's gun. The jamb just above her head splintered.

Tootie jerked back into the room. Hannigan reckoned the figure had either fired too quick or hadn't really wanted to kill her. A relieved sigh escaped his lips, whatever the case.

Hannigan, on his feet now, went for the Peacemaker at his hip, freeing it from its holster.

He half-stumbled, half-ran to the door, bracing himself against the jamb and waving Tootie back. He edged his head around, scanning the hallway, seeing it was empty.

A window was open at the end of the hall. Hannigan glanced at Tootie. 'You OK?'

She nodded. 'No extra holes I didn't come in with.'

Hannigan stepped out into the hall, keeping his back against a wall and sliding along it till he reached the window. He held the gun level with his face, finger ready on the trigger.

An outside stairway led to the street. With a short jump the attacker would have made it onto the landing easily. He now knew how the man had gotten into the hotel unseen, though not how he'd gotten into his room.

Hannigan took a cautious look

beyond the window, but couldn't see much in the darkness. The stairway led to an alley running alongside the hotel. He heard a horse burst into motion and knew the marauder was on his way out of town. Hannigan threw a leg over the sill and hopped onto the landing. He made his way down to the ground, but by the time he reached the street, the rider was disappearing into the distance.

He holstered his gun. He'd never be able to pick him off from this distance in the dark and by the time he fetched his horse — he saw no others in the street this time, all of them likely ridden to Trimble's flaming home — the rider would be long gone.

He gave a disgusted sigh, unhappy with himself for being taken so easily and even unhappier at the fact Tootie had nearly gotten her head shot off.

He made his way back down the alley and climbed the stairway to the window. Once back inside, he shut the window and returned to his room.

Closing the door, he saw Tootie sitting on the edge of the bed. She had fired the lantern and left her derringer on the bureau top, its load exhausted. She held up her hand; a slim piece of crimped metal glittering in the soft light.

'What's that?' Hannigan asked.

'Piece of metal, the kind some folks use to get into locked rooms. Works as a sort of makeshift skeleton key. They aren't hard to fashion.'

He nodded. 'You know that how?'

She shrugged, a smirk briefly touching her lips. 'Found it inside your room. He must have dropped it in the scuffle.'

Hannigan unbuckled his gunbelt and draped it over a brass bedpost. 'Wonder why he'd have that on him.'

She shrugged again, then rose to her feet and went to the door. 'Likely he was planning on sneaking into Trimble's office or house at some point.'

'Not house, that burned to the ground, with his compliments.'

'That where you were?'

He nodded. 'Just got back to find I had company.'

She offered a weak smile. 'Reckon I'll see you in the morning. Figure that's enough excitement for one night.'

'Tootie . . . ' He took a deep breath. Opening the door, she stood in the doorway. Her nightgown was powder-blue, with white lace highlighting the neckline, which was plunging. The material was sheer and hugged her slim figure. She was the most beautiful woman he had ever seen, except for the look of hurt in her eyes. She had risked her life to help him, would a hundred times over, no matter what he had said to her . . . or hadn't said.

'I don't need a week . . . ' he almost mumbled. Christ, things like this were damn near impossible for him. His heart started to pound and his palms dampened.

She tensed, as if steeling herself for something she was afraid to hear, a decision that would send her out of his life. 'Yes?' Her voice remained steady.

She was a strong woman. No one could take that away from her.

He went to the window, leaned a shoulder against the frame. 'I thought about it a lot since Revelation Pass. I would have left you that day . . . '

He heard her let out a slight gasp before he could finish. Finding the words were so hard that even good ones caused her more pain.

'But I wouldn't have got far. I would have come back for you, Tootie, like I said before. I meant it. I know that don't excuse what I tried to do. Nothing does. Not even me saying . . . I'm sorry.'

'It couldn't hurt . . . ' he heard her say, but little humor came with it.

He nodded. 'What would hurt would be waking up every morning knowing you weren't there because I made some foolish decision based on things that happened a long time ago . . . a decision made because I was a coward . . . '

'What are you saying?' She stepped

into the room, gently shutting the door behind her.

'I'm sayin' you want a promise from me, I'm willin' to give it. I won't leave long as you want me with you. I can't put it into words yet, so please don't make me try. I ain't a man who's gifted with saying what's inside him, but you know I'm a man who keeps his word.'

Her hand touched his shoulder and a sizzle of electricity went through him. 'I know you are . . . ' she whispered.

He turned to her, saw her eyes searching his, as if she were seeing everything that was Jim Hannigan, laying it bare. He took her in his arms, the feel of her body pressing to his, warm and giving, arousing sensations he'd never felt the likes of. 'I reckon there's some things I should tell you . . . '

'Shhh' she whispered, her head against his chest. 'It's enough for now. I won't ask you for more than you're ready to give.'

She pulled back and her lips found

his, the kiss deep and soul-stirring.

When she withdrew from his arms and went to the door, opening it, she looked back with a warm smile that might have graced an angel. She took her derringer from the bureau, then gently closed the door and left him, but this time the horrible feeling of emptiness wasn't there. Another feeling was, one he couldn't put into words but one that felt like a glimpse of Heaven to a Hell-bound man.

10

With the dawn came a renewed conviction on Jim Hannigan's part to track down Lessa Trimble's killer and settle the question of Galen's past misdeeds, if, indeed, the lawman had stepped over any lines, as the figure in black indicated. If Trimble had something to do with the Criggers' missing gold, then he had a lot to answer for.

He had to admit this new-found energy had a lot to do with Tootie. She'd reached something inside him, and with his promise to her last night a weight had come off his soul. It didn't mean he still wasn't going to fret over her safety and continue to try to talk her out of putting her life in jeopardy, but that was a trail he would ride when he came to it.

Hannigan dressed and headed out into the brightening morning. The sun rose in a fiery blaze, turning to brass by the time he devoured a quick breakfast of eggs and beefsteak washed down with a pot of Arbuckle's at the cafe.

By the time he reached the telegraph office the owner was just opening the door. The man wasn't particularly pleased to see Hannigan; a measure of fear danced in his eyes.

'Problem?' asked Hannigan, stepping up to the counter.

The man went behind a desk and took a yellow slip of paper from a drawer. 'This came for you, so I made sure nobody else got a look. This don't involve the marshal, does it?'

'Why would it matter to you?' Hannigan held the man's gaze. The operator licked his lips, eyelids fluttering.

'I sure don't need the grief if it does. This place is all I got. Don't want to be run out of town.'

A grim expression turned Hannigan's lips. 'That what happens to those who disagree with Trimble?'

The operator hesitated, then nodded. 'He'll know I let you send that message. He'll question me and likely his fists will do the talking. I ain't in the best of health. I won't be able to stand up to him.'

'Everyone in this town scared of the marshal that way?'

'Mostly. You know what happened to Pendelton, the liveryman?'

Hannigan nodded. 'I was there.'

'I don't want to be lying next to him in the boneyard.'

Hannigan came towards the desk, held out a hand. 'I won't let that happen. If Trimble's got sins to atone for, I'll see to it he does. Otherwise, I'll have the Territorial Marshal send someone down to make sure Trimble don't use intimidation on the folks here.'

'You can promise me he won't come after me?' The man's hand trembled as he passed Hannigan the slip.

Hannigan shook his head. 'I can't promise he won't, but I can promise that I'll do my best to stop it if he does.'

'Guess that will have to do.' The man wrapped bony arms about himself.

Hannigan peered at the slip in his hand, eyes scanning the words from his Pinkerton friend. Ice settled in his belly.

'Jesus . . . ' he whispered, the dark suspicion within him strengthening another notch. He looked up at the telegraph man and tipped a finger to his hat. The man settled into a chair behind the desk, sweat beading on his brow and little relief showing in his eyes.

He left the office, wondering where Trimble had spent the night, since his house had burned to the ground. He reckoned on one of two places, either in the saloon girl's room or at the marshal's office.

He decided on trying the saloon first, since it was closest, and open for breakfast. He strode along the board-walk, a handful of folks now about. Glancing into the distance, he could see a wispy black haze hanging over the ruins of the marshal's home. The odor of charred wood still hung in the air.

Reaching the saloon, he pushed through the batwings. The place held only a few patrons, their faces in their plates. The stale Durham smoke, heavy perfume and booze odors of the night before mixed with the scents of coffee and bacon. A couple of saloon girls doubled as waitresses, but he saw no sign of the Indian woman.

His first guess had been right. Trimble hunched over the bar, nursing a cup of coffee, an elbow jammed to the counter, a hand pressed to his forehead. A thin bandage was wrapped around the other hand, covering the rifle wound.

Hannigan came up behind the lawman, pulled out a stool and sat beside him.

'Whatta you want?' Trimble asked in an annoyed tone without even looking at him.

'Reckon it's time you came clean with me, Galen.' Hannigan signaled the 'keep for a cup of coffee. The 'keep poured him a cup and slid it onto the counter while Hannigan flipped two bits onto the polished bar.

After the 'keep walked away Trimble grunted, hand coming from his forehead to rest on the counter. 'Don't know what the hell you're getting at, but I'm in no mood to play games with you. My house burned to the ground, or didn't you notice that when you rode up last night?'

Hannigan took a sip of his coffee, then set the cup down. 'Joe Crigger wasn't responsible for that, or your wife's death. I got a notion we both know that.'

Trimble gazed at him with glassy bloodshot eyes. 'Course it was Crigger. January even described him.'

Hannigan was starting to wonder about that. The girl had painted a word picture of Crigger's face to a tee. That made her suddenly suspect, but he would let Tootie handle that angle. Reaching into his pocket, the manhunter brought out the telegram he'd received from his Pinkerton friend. He tossed it on the counter in front of Trimble. 'Joe Crigger's been dead three years. He tried robbing a train in Texas just across the Mex border and got his ass filled with lead for his troubles. His body was positively identified.'

'What?' Trimble shook his head, reading the slip that spat in the face of all obvious evidence. 'Ain't possible . . . ' His tone said he half didn't believe it, but also something else, that some sort of suspicion played in his mind, one he wasn't willing to share with Hannigan.

Hannigan shook his head. 'Whoever's behind that scarecrow mask isn't Joe Crigger. There's no mistake.'

Trimble glanced at Hannigan, then went silent, a storm brewing behind his eyes.

'What happened that day you brought the Crigger Gang down, Galen?'

Trimble shrugged. 'You already know. Read the accounts in the pulp novels. They got it right.'

'Did they? I reckon they got right

what you told them, but you didn't tell them everything, did you?'

'You accusin' me of being a liar, Hannigan?'

'For the moment I'm accusing you of withholding. Give me the story in your own words. Convince me you ain't involved in somethin' shady that somebody wants you to pay for.'

'I don't owe you nothin', Hannigan. Get the hell out of my town.'

'You can tell it to me or I can get a territorial marshal down here to investigate.'

Trimble shuddered with suppressed rage. Hannigan wasn't sure the man wasn't going to try taking another poke at him. After dragging minutes of silence Trimble sighed, then said, 'Like I told the papers and those book writers, I cornered the Crigger Gang in an old house outside of Orchard Town. There was a shoot out. Me and Trip were hunkered down too well, though. During a lull I managed to set fire to the place.'

'How'd you set fire to it?' Hannigan had a notion he knew.

Trimble let out a small sound of disgust. 'Same way that masked rider set fire to mine last night.'

'They came runnin' out?'

'Yeah . . . yeah, they did.'

'Hands in the air?'

Trimble didn't answer.

Hannigan's belly cinched. 'You shot them down like mad dogs, didn't you?'

Trimble squirmed. 'They came out guns blazing. I had no choice.'

Something in Trimble's voice put a lie to his words. Hannigan saw the scenario in his mind. The gang had surrendered, not come out fighting, all except for Joe, who had gone out the back and managed to escape. Trimble had shot the men down in cold blood, instead of bringing them in for trial. It put a sour taste in his mouth, but he reckoned he couldn't feel much sympathy for a band of cutthroats like the Criggers, especially ones who had brutally murdered Trimble's fiancée.

'Reckon I can't judge you for it.' Hannigan took another sip from his coffee.

'You're still callin' me a liar, Hannigan.'

'I'm callin' what you did understandable to a point. What about Trip, how did he figure into it?'

'Trip, well, Trip got over-eager. He went up to one of the Criggers who lay bleeding in the dirt. He didn't see the fella had managed to hold onto his gun. He shot Trip point blank.'

'You saw him die?'

'Hell, I buried him, like I told you before. Why you askin' me all these questions, Hannigan? Ain't nothing different than what you knew before.'

Except for the knowledge of the gang's defenseless slaughter, but it made little difference in the case as far as Hannigan could tell.

'What about the Crigger gold?' Hannigan watched the marshal's reaction closely.

Trimble flinched, but recovered quickly. 'Don't know what you mean, Hannigan,' Trimble mumbled with little conviction.

'I think you know exactly what I mean, Galen. See, last night I got myself a visit from our rider friend. He told me to ask you about the Crigger gold. Rumor had it they had a huge stash of bullion and loot from their robberies. That money was never found. Those men didn't get the chance to spend it before you killed them, did they? And Joe Crigger couldn't have rode out with it.'

'Hannigan, I swear you best shut your goddamn mouth now before I do it for you.' Trimble glared at him, fury in his eyes.

'I reckon you just answered my question, Galen. You found that stash, didn't you? Used it to build that fancy house of yours, buy your way into being the hero of this town. And someone else besides Joe Crigger knows that.'

Trimble jumped off his stool like a spring uncoiling. He launched a powerful swing at Hannigan, but his balance wasn't what it might have been, likely from the effects of the previous night's events and probably a hangover atop that.

The blow whisked over Hannigan's head as he ducked and came sideways off his stool. The momentum threw Trimble off balance and Hannigan swept a foot back, connecting behind the marshal's knees while he jammed a fist into the lawdog's chest. The marshal hit the floor with a crash. Patrons looked over, but seemed little concerned about the lawman's dilemma.

The marshal glared up at Hannigan. 'You pushed me for the last time, you sonofabitch. I don't care what we were back then. You'll pay for making a fool of me in front of my town.'

Hannigan gazed down at him, face tight. 'That's the second time you threatened me, Galen, and the second time you ain't backed it up to my face. You want to get it done, now's your chance.'

Trimble didn't move. His eyes narrowed a fraction and his sights remained fixed on Hannigan, but he made no attempt to climb to his feet to accept the challenge.

'That's what I thought,' the man-hunter said. 'You change your mind, I'll be around. And for the record, I think you're lying about something important. Don't rightly know what at this point, but I'll figure it out. When I do you best hope your involvement in whatever it was holds up in a court.'

Hannigan backed away, keeping an eye on Trimble until he was through the batwings. He paused in the morning sunlight, then started walking along the boardwalk, mind indexing what Trimble had told him. Damn little, was his conclusion, but Trimble was still hiding something; Hannigan was sure of it. Joe Crigger was dead. The outlaw could not be the man behind the mask, no matter how it looked, no matter what the bargirl had told them. The girl was lying, too, but why? For Trimble? Hannigan got the notion that wasn't the case, based on the impression he'd gotten of her the night he'd floored

Trimble and the look she'd cast him after Pendelton's death. Maybe Tootie could coax a reason out of her tonight.

If not Joe Crigger, then who? Who else had been directly involved in the events of the day? Nobody Hannigan knew about. Crigger and Trip Matterly were dead. Clara Matterly was dead, and Hannigan recollected Galen telling him Trip had no other kin. Same with Lessa. She was an orphan, no family; that much she'd told him on her wedding day.

Trimble had stolen the fortune amassed by the Crigger Gang; that much was now clear. That in itself painted Trimble as a crooked lawman, but proving it was another matter. They weren't about to get the masked rider on a witness stand testifying to the fact and Trimble had likely made sure no trails to the money remained.

That rider. Try as Hannigan might attribute him to just some no-good who had read the tale and wanted to make a name for himself, he couldn't make it wash. Something about it rang too personal, too passion-driven. The figure wanted Trimble to atone for an unknown crime, not to provide him with a reputation.

That left no one else. Crigger was dead, his body positively identified. Trip Matterly was dead; Trimble had seen him die, buried the body himself . . .

A suspicion pricked Hannigan. Trimble had lied about the way he brought down the gang; Trimble had lied about finding the Crigger loot.

A chill rode down Hannigan's back. Had he lied about the way Matterly died?

Why?

Because it was his fault . . .

The thought rose unbidden in Hannigan's mind but he couldn't rightly see how it would make a difference to the case. Unless someone else had witnessed the killing, someone with a personal interest in Matterly?

The more Hannigan struggled to piece it together the more it frustrated him. His manhunter's intuition told him he had a fragment of something, but that was it.

Trip Matterly . . .

Again the name rang in his mind. 'Why, dammit?' he muttered. Lies . . . Trimble had lied about important details, ones that made him look better. That was typical of the man Jim Hannigan had known, if extreme.

His mind searched his memories from those days, the three of them working together, Matterly specifically. The schemer of the three, he had told Tootie. Always thinking something he wasn't saying . . .

'Christ . . . ' Hannigan whispered, something taking shape in his mind he didn't want to believe. Had Matterly been in on it with Trimble somehow? Planned to keep all that gold?

Or was he s'posed to be and Trimble had found a way to cut him out?

Would that mean Trimble was responsible for Matterly's death?

'Ask him about Crigger gold . . . ' the

figure had said. A plan of revenge . . .

Who else would know about the gold?

Trip Matterly.

Dead. Killed by Trimble?

Hannigan stopped, a distasteful notion occurring to him the more Matterly's name weighed on his mind. A small groan escaped his lips, but the suspicion inside was strengthening and he needed to put an answer to it. However, it involved a grisly task on a slim connecting thread of circumstance and thought. If a bullet had brought Matterly down, did it match a Crigger weapon or Trimble's? Any chance at proving that — and it was slim, Hannigan reckoned — meant getting the bullet out of Matterly's body, then exhuming one of the Crigger bodies and trying to match slugs. That might prove Trimble a murderer and settle one part of the case, though it still left the identity of the dark rider a mystery.

At the moment it was his only lead. In motion again, he steeled himself for the task that would prove or disprove his suspicions regarding Trimble once and for all. He hoped he was wrong.

Stopping briefly at the hotel, he wrote out a note for Tootie, asking her to work on the bargirl, January, then sealed it in an envelope and left it with the hotel clerk to give to her when she got back from the schoolhouse.

A half hour later, Jim Hannigan pushed aside the rusty gate leading to the Hollow Pass Cemetery. Locating a shovel in a small tool shed, after pounding off the old lock with a handy stone, he made his way down the rows of graves until he came to Trip Matterly's marker.

Christ, Hannigan, this might be the lowest you've sunk on a case. Trimble used to be a friend. You ready to face the worst about him?

Trimble had lied . . . more than once. But was he a cold-blooded killer where a friend was concerned, instead of outlaws? Had Hannigan ever really known the man? Had Trimble hidden a darker side of himself all that time they rode together, one just waiting to throw off the restraints when the opportunity presented itself?

He plunged the shovel into the earth. It took more than an hour to reach the wooden top of the coffin, then another half hour to exhume enough dirt around it so he would be able to get the lid up while standing in the grave. He tossed the shovel out of the hole then jumped out himself and went back to the tool shed. Finding an iron bar he could use to pry off the lid, he drew a deep breath and gathered his strength.

Sweat streamed down his face and soaked his shirt as he went back to the grave. Dirt soiled his clothing and face. The noon-day sun had brought the day to an uncomfortable temperature, which didn't help matters.

He hopped into the grave, then gazed at the dirt-encrusted lid. 'Forgive me, Trip,' he whispered, taking a breath, then jamming the bar into the crack between lid and box. Nails came loose with the shriek of a dying beast as Hannigan pried. He wedged the bar along the lid, getting the front half and most of the side lifted enough to grip. Tossing the bar to the ground above, he bent, grasping the edges of the lid and straightening. The rest of the nails pulled free, the wood rotted enough to pose little resistance.

He pushed back the lid, letting it lie against the opposite side and looked into the coffin, bracing himself for the sight of Matterly's decomposed body.

★　★　★

Tootie had gotten Hannigan's note explaining all he'd discovered about the Crigger brother and pinpointing the marshal and January both as liars. She had spent the entire morning at the schoolhouse, posing as Pauline Twily, providing learning to a room full of children not the least bit happy to be back to the books. Although she had dreaded it, the morning went by fast enough and by two o'clock she found herself dressed in her bargirl get-up, blond tresses tumbling about her shoulders and a derringer tucked into her bodice. Getting out in daylight wasn't going to be as easy as after dark, so she took a page from the rider's book and slid out the hall window onto the outside stairway. She managed to make it to the street without being seen and those who saw her beyond that point had no idea where she came from.

Going to the saloon she found it virtually deserted, the 'keep having stepped out to do bank business and January sitting on a stool watching the place. The other girls were likely sleeping off last's night's business.

'You're early.' January's dark eyes widened a bit. She had likely picked up on something on Tootie's face that told her there was a reason Tootie had come in before her shift.

Tootie threaded her way through the tables until she reached the girl at the counter. 'You and me, we're going to have a little talk and I want the truth.'

The dark-haired woman studied Tootie's face, her own features tightening. 'Who are you really? You're no bargirl.'

'I'd say the same about you if I hadn't seen you take the marshal to your bed.'

'I do what has to be done . . . ' Her voice lowered, disgust in her eyes.

'You got a reason for being with him, don't you?'

'Reckon I don't know what you're talkin' about.'

'The description you gave of the man who attacked you . . . '

'What about it?' The girl appeared suddenly a little nervous, though she struggled to hide it.

Tootie decided to press the dove, put her cards on the table. 'That fella's dead. Killed three years ago. He couldn't have been in your room. Someone else was and I think you know who.'

The girl looked away, this time

unable to hide the anxiety in her eyes. 'You're working with that manhunter, Hannigan, aren't you? I ain't seen you take a man upstairs since you got here. Fact, I've seen you fend off advances. Puzzled me at the time but it makes sense now.' She turned back to Tootie, her expression daring her to deny it.

Tootie nodded, figuring if she came clean the girl was more likely to trust her. 'I play a part. I wouldn't go so far it disgraced him.'

The anxiety changed to sadness, regret, maybe. 'I had no choice.'

'Who is he, the man who came to your room?'

The girl shook her head. 'He's nobody you need to know about. He won't hurt you or Hannigan if you stay out of his way. He just wants Trimble.'

'He hurt Trimble's wife.'

'It couldn't be helped. She . . . '

'Was innocent.'

The girl didn't take it any further, just tensed, her gaze suddenly jerking to the batwings.

Tootie turned. A man stood there, gun in hand, eyes glazed with anger. He stepped down the three steps to the saloon proper and came towards them. 'You know, January, I figured you and me had somethin', but I come to find out you've been lying to me.'

January shook her head, genuine fear now in her eyes. 'No, Galen, I ain't lied about nothin'.'

'I figured it out soon enough after Hannigan told me Joe Crigger was dead. But I'll deal with you later.' His gaze shifted to Tootie. His hand suddenly darted out, grabbing her blonde hair and yanking it free to reveal her own dark tresses confined by pins and a hairnet beneath the wig. The marshal flung the wig aside. 'It took me a while, but I finally realized where we'd met. That first night here in the saloon, then the morning outside the general store. Tootie or Pauline or whoever you are. One thing's plain: You're in this with Hannigan. He planted you here to ruin me.'

A defiant look hardened Tootie's face. 'He has nothing to do with me getting this job. I chose to be here. But you ruined yourself, from what I can see. I'm just lookin' to catch a killer.'

'Are you, now?' He motioned with his gun. 'Step away from her.' He indicated January, who stepped back, worry in her eyes.

Tootie stood her ground, determined not to back down to him. 'You best just tell what you know, Marshal. We both know it wasn't Crigger who came back for you.'

Trimble lashed out with his gun hand. The blow took her clean in the mouth, sending welts of pain splintering through her teeth. Her head whirled and she went sideways, legs giving out beneath her. She hit the sawdust-covered floor hard, instantly struggled to get back up, unsuccessful.

'That's what I gave my no-good whore of a wife when she backtalked me.' Trimble stepped over to her.

'Reckon you deserve no better.'

Tootie glared up at him, blood dribbling from her broken lip. Her hand started for her bodice. The marshal was faster than she expected. He lunged, jammed a hand down her top and grabbed the derringer before she could get to it. Straightening, he flung the gun across the bar room.

'You'll have to do better than that, Missy . . . ' He sent a fist into her face. Blackness swept in and stopped time for an instant. Then she was blearily staring up at the chandelier, pain radiating through her entire face, muscles unable to function. She heard the marshal's voice cut above the pounding roar in her mind.

'I don't know what connection you got in this, January,' he said, 'but I'll be back to find out after I get through with Hannigan. You best be here if you don't want me tracking you down like a dog and blowing your head off.' He looked down at Tootie, who saw his face jittering before her vision. 'I'll be back for you, too. Reckon then I'll find out just what Hannigan finds special enough about you to give up working alone. Don't you go nowhere, you hear?' He uttered a laugh, holstered his gun, then left the bar.

Tootie struggled to get back up. January knelt beside her, shoving an arm beneath hers to help her up.

'Don't worry, he'll pay for what he's done soon enough. You and Hannigan just got to let it happen.'

Tootie tried to shake off the cobwebs, staggering, then collapsed again. 'I ain't gonna just let him kill Jim . . . ' she said, will taking over. She crawled to where Trimble had kicked her derringer and picked it up, stuffing it back into her bodice top. Wiping a dribble of blood from her lips, she managed to reach her feet on her own this time. She braced herself against a table, gasping deep breaths, then staggered towards the batwings.

She was barely aware of January heading out the back way.

Jim Hannigan set a hardbacked chair beside the marshal's desk, facing the door. He lowered himself into it, to await Trimble's return. The lawman would come back here sooner or later and when he did he was going to answer some hard questions.

If Hannigan read him right by now he'd likely be building a healthy worry over whether the manhunter would piece together the events of that day long ago. He'd be worried his career as a hero might come to a disgraceful end. And while Hannigan held nothing concrete, he now had a notion exactly who the killer was, if not all the answers why.

Hannigan's face was still smudged with dirt and his shirt soaked with sweat. He drew his Peacemaker, held it in his lap. Trimble was volatile, likely riled to a point of rage after their last encounter. Hannigan wouldn't give the lawdog the chance to do to him what he had done to the liveryman.

The door suddenly burst open and Trimble stopped on the threshold, a gun leveled in his hand. He eyed Hannigan, fury in his gaze.

'Come in, Trimble. Close the door.' Hannigan hadn't expected the man to have a weapon drawn. That meant something had pushed Trimble to the edge and he had decided to do something about Hannigan getting close before it became a bigger problem than it already was.

Trimble shut the door, keeping his attention fixed on the manhunter. 'I went lookin' for you at the hotel. Clerk hadn't seen you but when I asked around Horace said he saw you lettin' yourself into my office.'

Hannigan nodded. 'I guessed as much from the gun in your hand. Reckon you intend on doin' more than askin' me to join you for dinner.'

Trimble stepped further into the office. The afternoon sun was starting to sink towards the distant mountains, giving the room a preternatural gloom. Weird shadows and softening light filled the office.

'Why'd you come here?' Trimble's voice came low, but Hannigan could hear the suppressed fury behind the question.

'Something's come to light since our talk.'

'Yeah, what's that?' Trimble's gun remained steady on Hannigan. The manhunter bet he could still get his own Peacemaker up and take out Trimble, even if the man's bullet found him.

'Trip Matterly.'

Trimble tensed, stepping a bit deeper into the room. 'What about old Trip?' His voice carried a hitch.

'Either he climbed out of his grave when you weren't lookin' or you're lying about a Crigger killing him that day.'

Trimble surveyed Hannigan, likely noting the dirt on his face and stained shirt. 'You dug up the coffin?'

Hannigan nodded. 'Funny thing is, I just planned on retrieving the bullet that killed him. Imagine my surprise when I discovered that box empty.'

Trimble stuttered a sigh. 'You got a notion what happened, I reckon?'

'I got lots of notions, Galen. And I don't care for none of them.'

'You figured I killed Trip.'

'Maybe you shot Trip that day but I reckon you didn't kill him.'

'Bravo, Mr Hannigan,' came a voice from the back of the office. Both men's heads turned toward the source of the sound, a figure in black who stood with a leveled Smith & Wesson. The killer had come in soundlessly, Hannigan and Trimble's attention too fixated on their own standoff to notice. 'I came in the back way, hope you don't mind, Trimble.'

'Trip . . . ?' Trimble peered at the figure wearing the scarecrow mask, as if trying to see beneath the disguise.

'Put your gun on the desk.' The dark figure motioned with his gun.

Trimble hesitated, aim still on Hannigan.

'You can shoot Hannigan if you want, Galen, but I'll still kill you.'

Trimble seemed to think it over, then set his gun on the desktop.

'You, too, Hannigan,' ordered the figure.

Hannigan eased the gun from his lap, placed it on the desk. He stood, turning halfway towards the figure.

'How'd you come to be here?' Trimble asked. Beads of sweat had sprung out on his forehead. His face had reddened. He was a step away from charging the figure, Hannigan reckoned.

'January came and got me, told me you were onto her and going after Hannigan. I figured it was as good a time as any to make you disgrace yourself before you go to your grave.'

'He didn't kill you that day, Matterly, did he?' asked Hannigan, mind racing to try to keep the man talking until he could inch close enough to have a chance at grabbing the figure's gun.

The figure laughed, one hand going to his mask and yanking it free. Hannigan saw the features of the man he'd thought long dead, the face more deeply creased, the circles beneath his eyes blacker, but no less recognizable.

'Not for lack of trying.' Matterly glared at Trimble.

'What happened?' asked Hannigan.

'We brought down the Criggers but not the way Trimble said in those newspaper articles and books. I read them all, by the way, Galen. Every last one of 'em telling how big a hero you were and how poor Trip Matterly had given his life in the line of duty. I reckon you gave me a nice funeral?' Matterly laughed without humor. 'No matter.' His gaze went back to the manhunter. 'Trimble set their place afire and shot them down as they came out waving bandannas to surrender. Left a bad taste in my mouth but I reckon I didn't care about the gang. I cared about my sister, Clara.'

Hannigan nodded. 'No regrets for a gang that killed her.'

''Cept they didn't kill her, did they, Galen?' Matterly pinned the lawdog with his gaze.

Hannigan's belly plunged. 'She was found like the other women they murdered . . . '

Matterly's attention went back to the manhunter. 'Yeah, she was, but why don't you ask Trimble how she got that way?' Trimble's face had gone white by now, though fury still seethed behind his eyes. 'Not feeling like a braggart so much now, Galen? Too bad.'

'What the hell do you mean, Matterly?' Hannigan didn't like the thoughts locking together in his mind.

'Clara left a diary, told how Trimble had been mistreating her. Said she had fears he'd kill her because she wanted to break their engagement. Said she planned to tell him she was leavin' the very day she went missing. I confronted Trimble with it, right after we got that gang. He denied it but I could tell he was lying. I called him on it, told him he was seen leaving her body in that field. He pulled a gun and shot me. Funny thing was, I was plannin' on doing the same to him as soon as I got him to admit her death was his fault.'

'Yet you aren't dead,' Hannigan said.

'He left me lying there while he went back to town to fetch a funeral wagon. Thought I was bleeding my last. January found me. She was one of the Criggers' whores. She dragged me off, fixed me up. Took more than year before I could function right. Damn near died just the way he wanted.'

Hannigan's gaze went to Trimble, his features confirming everything Trip had said. 'You faked his burial, so nobody would know. Then made up a story about how the Criggers killed him.'

Trimble's body trembled with rage. 'I figured you crawled off and died somewhere, Trip. Figured animals got your corpse.' The words came laced with spite for the man holding the gun on him.

'Then he took the loot the Criggers kept in a root cellar, and set himself up as king of this town. He took Clara from me, Hannigan, killed my sister. You can see now why he has to pay for that?'

Hannigan nodded. 'Let me take him in, Trip. He'll hang for it.'

Trip Matterly uttered a sharp laugh. 'I'd hang, too, Hannigan. I did kill his wife, after all. There's still laws against that even for purposes of revenge. No, his time has come to pay for what he did — '

Hannigan acted then, before Matterly had even finished his words. The manhunter was certain not only would Matterly kill Trimble but he would have to kill him as well, or risk being chased down.

Hannigan dove sideways, making a grab for Trip's gun hand, getting it.

A shot blasted and a bullet whined towards Trimble. Hannigan had managed to deflect Trip's aim just enough so that the bullet missed the marshal and plowed into the wall behind him.

The manhunter tried to wrench the gun from Matterly's grip, but the man was stronger than Hannigan expected. Trip jerked his hand free, tried to aim again at Trimble.

Hannigan snapped an uppercut that clacked from Matterly's chin. The killer staggered.

Another shot rang out, crashing like caged thunder in the small room.

Matterly jerked, froze a moment. The gun fell from his nerveless fingers. Then he collapsed into a heap at Hannigan's feet. This time Trip Matterly wouldn't recover from his wound. He was dead the instant Trimble's bullet punched into his heart.

Hannigan turned to see Trimble smiling slightly, gun smoking in his hand. The marshal triggered three more shots, each bullet drilling into the dead form of Trip Matterly.

After he finished, Trimble looked at Hannigan. 'Won't come back this time . . . ' he muttered.

'I'll have your badge for this, Galen,' said Hannigan.

'No, you won't. Because you see, there was a struggle and Trip killed you before I killed him. Sad, really.'

Hannigan's eyes narrowed. He was close enough to the desk to make a grab for his gun, but not close enough to get it up and leveled before Trimble ended his life.

'You're forgetting Trip showing up after all this time will raise some questions. You're ruined as a lawman any way you feed it to them.'

'I'll think of something. I'm good at that.' Trimble shook his head. 'You should have just taken my advice and left, Hannigan, but it's better this way. You always were a threat to my limelight.'

'You're mad, Galen.'

'You're dead, Hannigan.'

The door burst open behind the marshal. Hannigan's gaze jerked in that direction. Tootie stood in the doorway, derringer in hand. She instantly took in the situation, saw the threat. She triggered both barrels into the marshal as he brought his gun around.

The bullets didn't stop him. He jerked, wavered, but his gun still came about and in fractions of a moment Tootie would be dead.

Hannigan reacted from instinct, letting his years of experience take over. He lunged to the desk, grabbed his sawed-off Peacemaker.

Trimble had nearly made it all the way around.

Tootie froze where she stood.

Hannigan whisked the gun up, leveling it in one fluid motion on Trimble. He triggered all six bullets. Each took Trimble in the back, kicked him forward in ragdoll fashion. He hit the wall, rebounded, the gun tumbling from his grip. He slammed into the floor, unmoving. Blood pooled beneath his body and spread across the wood. A rasping breath escaped his lungs, then nothing further.

Hannigan looked over at Tootie, who

offered a thin smile. 'Seems I'm always saving your ass . . . '

'Hope you don't live to regret it.'

* * *

The saloon was starting to fill. The 'keep stood behind the counter, wiping out glasses. January sat at a table by herself, a whiskey bottle before her, the cap off. Hannigan paused just inside the batwings, watching the woman take a swig, then set the bottle down.

She cast Hannigan a glance as he came down the three steps and crossed the room to her table. He pulled out a chair and lowered himself onto it.

'He's dead, ain't he?' Her voice carried little emotion.

'Yes.' Hannigan's voice was a whisper.

'Trimble?' Spite coated the marshal's name.

'Him, too.'

'He got what he deserved.'

'Reckon he did.'

A tear slipped down the girl's cheek and her lips quivered. 'He was fine at first, you know.'

'Trip?'

She nodded. 'Trip. Thought everything would be all right. I didn't have to cater to the whims of those Criggers no more. I was glad they were dead because I saw what they did to women once they got tired of them. But I didn't know that 'fore I hooked up with Joe, and then it was too late to get out. They would have left me hanging there like Trimble's wife sooner or later. After I nursed Trip back to health I figured we'd have a life. It was going to be a new start.'

'But he couldn't let go of what Trimble did to his sister.'

'Everyday he just seemed to fret over it. Like he was always thinking on it but not saying nothing. Got worse as the years passed. Part my fault, I reckon. I could see it building but I kept telling myself nothing would come of it and one day he'd let it go. 'Cept one day he came out with it, said he was gonna take Trimble down in pieces, ruin him, then kill him. I tried to talk him out of it.'

'But his mind wasn't right.'

Her eyes searched his, pain within them, tears shimmering. 'Reckon it wasn't.'

'Why'd you let yourself be used by Trimble?'

'Trip . . . forced me, said he'd leave me if I didn't help him. I was s'posed to get close to Trimble, keep him busy when need be, lead him to his death at Trip's hands when the time came. He was going to show Trimble what it felt like to be betrayed then shot.'

'Surely you knew you'd have to compromise yourself. Trip had to know, too.'

She nodded. 'I loved him, Mr Hannigan. I couldn't lose him no matter what. So I let Trimble . . . touch me. Trip . . . he knew, but his plan was more important to him.'

'It consumed him enough to place

his woman in a position no sane man would have asked, and made him kill an innocent woman as well.'

'I didn't want him to hurt her. I came into town days before, got set up here. I saw her a few times, getting supplies at the general store. The kids, they followed her like she was their mom. I liked her, though I didn't know her.'

'Yet you let her be killed.'

'I couldn't talk him out of it. I couldn't talk him out of anything.'

'That makes you an accessory. I'll have to bring you in.'

She nodded. 'I know. I expected as much.'

'I'll talk to the judge, make sure he knows you were forced into some of it. I reckon they might go easier on you. It's the most I can do.'

'I'm obliged.'

Hannigan stood, offered the woman his hand. She took it, standing. He led her to the batwings. Tootie stood just inside them now, dressed in riding clothes, her dark hair free of the net.

The Indian girl looked at her. 'Tootie . . . '

Tootie nodded. 'Angela's my real name.'

'Angela . . . ' the girl whispered. She looked at Hannigan then back to Tootie. 'You're a lucky woman, you know that, don't you? Your man . . . he won't ask you to do the things . . . '

Tootie nodded. 'I know. Reckon I am.'

They led her outside where Tootie had three horses waiting.

THE END

We do hope that you have enjoyed reading this large print book.

Did you know that all of our titles are available for purchase?

We publish a wide range of high quality large print books including:
Romances, Mysteries, Classics
General Fiction
Non Fiction and Westerns

Special interest titles available in large print are:
The Little Oxford Dictionary
Music Book, Song Book
Hymn Book, Service Book

Also available from us courtesy of Oxford University Press:
Young Readers' Dictionary
(large print edition)
Young Readers' Thesaurus
(large print edition)

For further information or a free brochure, please contact us at:
Ulverscroft Large Print Books Ltd.,
The Green, Bradgate Road, Anstey,
Leicester, LE7 7FU, England.
Tel: (00 44) **0116 236 4325**
Fax: (00 44) **0116 234 0205**

Other titles in the
Linford Western Library:

HARD RIDE TO LARGO

Jack Holt

When Jack Danner arrived in Haley Ridge he spent the night in jail. But then financier Spencer Bonnington offers him fifteen hundred dollars to escort Sarah, his niece, to her father's ranch in Largo. However, their journey is fraught with danger, especially when Bob Rand and his partners see Sarah as a prize and a means of ransom from the Bonningtons. Danner is being watched, but by whom? An easy fifteen hundred becomes the hardest money he's ever earned.

MOON RAIDERS

Skeeter Dodds

Wayne Creek is a family town, not overly prosperous. However, when Samuel Lane arrives with his own enrichment in mind, change is anticipated. Though the town might find affluence through him, it would also become dangerous, with the dregs of the West flooding in . . . Standing alone against Lane is Jeb Tierney. The scales of justice seem to be loaded against him — and yet nothing is quite as it seems. Will Lane, after all, get his much-deserved comeuppance?

THE SHERIFF OF RED ROCK

H. H. Cody

Jake Helsby figured there would be trouble as the rider headed into town. It had started when somebody put a piece of lead into Fred at his place, the Circle B. One of the hands reckoned the Grissom kid was responsible, but Jake was suspicious of the mayor's anxiety to hang the suspect, and of Lily Jeffords's interest in the kid's well-being. And even as he searched for the true culprit, Jake had his own dark secret to protect . . .